merrow

Ananda
Braxton-Smith

CANDLEWICK PRESS

Copyright © 2010 by Ananda Braxton-Smith

First U.S. edition 2016

Library of Congress Catalog Card Number pending
ISBN 978-0-7636-7924-8

16 17 18 19 20 21 BVG 10 9 8 7 6 5 4 3 2 1

Printed in Berryville, VA, U.S.A.

This book was typeset in Garamond.

Candlewick Press
99 Dover Street
Somerville, Massachusetts 02144

visit us at www.candlewick.com

For Nigel,
my own true Northman

A NOTE FROM THE AUTHOR

Some of the words in this book are Manx, the talk of the people of Isle of Man in the Irish Sea. This language nearly died out but is now reviving. There are still only two thousand speakers of it in the world.

The language of the Vikings is called Old Norse. The author would like to thank Ruarigh Dale of the Centre for the Study of the Viking Age at the University of Nottingham, U.K., for giving Ulf words.

CHAPTER ONE

Wrack

AUNTIE USHAG SAID I WASN'T FIT to be around. She said it was beyond her how a body could be so prickly and dark. She said it gave her the Screaming Purples just to look at me, always lying around looking sideways at her like a reptile on a hot rock. That if I couldn't raise myself on my hind legs and help, the least I could do was go away and leave her to it.

Honor Bright, all I said was I wished she'd open her mind a bit and that she didn't know all about everything. I said she couldn't prove that our Marrey great-grandmother wasn't a merrow. She couldn't swear that Mam had run away after Pa drowned, now, could she? All I said was perhaps Mam had actually just gone home to her people under the sea, and that she could come back to us one day, if she wanted to. I only said it was possible.

"What you don't witness with your eyes, don't witness with your mouth," my aunt snapped. She could be as tight-minded and purse-mouthed as the southerners she hated so. These days she was as touchy as a slug, and wholly unreasonable. I slipped out the window with her still wittering on behind me, and was nearly away when she shouted, "Never mind me opening the mind. What about you opening and using the door?"

That woman had eyes in the back of her head. "And fetch some garlic if you can spare the time."

I headed for the cows.

In the byre I filled my stomach with warm, foamy milk straight from Breck. Bo lowed softly and butted me, gentle but determined as always. I rested my head on hers, smelling her warmth and listening to the crunch and creak as she ate. She was only a calf, and I loved that we could stand head to head and eye to eye. As we stood that way, I felt some of her steadiness pass into me. There's nothing more peaceful than a happy cow.

All winter I'd been tormented by these restless humors. My legs itched inside, and I just had to walk. It was the only thing that helped. I walked through icy wind and sleet, storms and thunder, and those days that sulk about in grey garments and sighs. Each day, I walked farther and found more of Carrick's hidden places. I was sure Auntie Ushag knew nothing of these warm hollows filled with dry leaves and molted fur, or those caves up the gorge where bats hang all day like drying kelp. Life was all work to her. She probably knew only the yard and her trapping trails, and the cove.

I was sure she knew nothing of the little inlet tucked into the cove's cliff walls. Its white sand and green water, its climbers and dangling vines appeared to me a kind of impossible paradise. I could see all the way to its sandy seabed and even make out the schools of tiny fish and deep drifting weed. I heard the inlet call to me; I knew it was my own, my very own, but I couldn't find a way to get down the sheer face. All I could do was stand on the cliff and look as the inlet beach whispered and gleamed.

We have always had days when this island floats in an edgeless blue world. When I was young, they'd been easy days to be happy, but now everything was wrong. The sun was too hot, the sky was too blue, the dawn birds screamed at the blinding sun, and the cows bored or bullied me. All talk ended in trouble, and Auntie Ushag and I were strangers.

Even the island had grown restless. We had been rocked by earthshakes all through fall and winter. In our cove, the cliff had been quietly slipping into the sea, rock by rock and stone by stone. Summer had been calm, but the very ground now had this pent-up quality, and we lived with one eye on the cliffs. I didn't mind. It suited my humor, which was full of dark predictions and trouble.

"Go away"! I couldn't remember Ushag ever telling me to go away before. No mam, no pa, and now this aunt who didn't want to claim me. I was an orphan. Why had I never noticed how sour Ushag was? It was baffling how much of a spit hag she'd become in just a few months.

That morning, all I'd done was tell her about my dream, and she couldn't have looked more buffeted if I'd turned into a fish before her face. She turned grey and pressed her lips together as if she wanted to stop them forming words.

It was only a dream, I told her.

In it, the sea was getting green in the light of morning, and I was on the shore collecting limpets. Everything was as it always is, calm and unremarkable; then I saw out in the cove a pale round moon rippling just under the water and closing in on the shore. I prickled all over but couldn't look away.

When the moon thing reached the shallows, it drew itself out of the purple sea and bobbed there, half in, half out, letting me look. The torso of a greenish woman rose out of the foam, paler than any woman I ever saw. It seemed transparent, and I thought I saw the blue veins pulsing in its neck and breasts. Its flowing hair seemed to be an ocean in itself, so flapping was it with tiny silver fish. I stepped into the water up to my knees to see it better.

I saw its tail then, shining and coiling under the surface, and I knew it to be a merrow. Raising my eyes to its face, I was shocked to see tears dropping from eyes singularly wild and hollow. I suppose I'd never thought of the merrows as having mortal feelings. I suppose I'd thought of them as glamorous fish, but cold and heartless. This one seemed to be full of a heart that was breaking. Wading in up to my thighs, I lifted my hand toward the wet, weeping creature.

It called me by name.

"Neen." My blood ran cold as a winter stream.

Twice it called. "Nee-een."

A third time.

"Nee-eenie," it called me, doleful-like and lonely. Reaching with webbed fingers through the sea spray, it dropped a sizable pearl into my hand. There was something about its face I knew from somewhere. Then it turned and was gone, with no trace of bubbles to mark a trail. I was left on the shore, gripping the pearl and searching for the wake.

Then I woke up.

After my aunt's first reaction, during which I thought she was going to be sick, she'd pulled herself together and asked who'd been telling me those stories.

"What stories?" I asked.

"Merrows, water horses, charmers . . . all of that." She rolled her eyes to the sky as though petitioning someone there for patience, and I felt myself grow still and colder even than the dream merrow's touch.

"Nobody told me, I just heard," I said. "What's a water horse?"

"It's nothing, is what it is." She gave me a sharp, sudden glance. "You can't have just heard. Somebody has been filling your head."

I thought how typical it was that she would take it for granted that I had a head that needed to be filled with stuff, as if it were hollow. As if I had no head already filled with its own stuff. I felt overhot and shifty, and before I knew it, I was saying all that about opening her mind a bit and not knowing everything about everything.

Auntie Ushag did not like me saying such things.

"And you, heishan, you know nothing about any-thing." She came close and pulled herself up to her full height, but because for the last few months we've been the same height, it didn't have the effect she was looking for. In fact, we both noticed at the same time that I had to look down to meet her eyes. She took a big breath, fattening herself up like a puffer fish. "The trouble with you is that you're neither one thing nor the other," she added. "You're an in-between."

I didn't know what that was. It sounded like an insult.

"You're in between your own self," she said.

"What does that mean?" I asked, but she'd finished with conversing. She said all that about reptiles and darkness, and then she shouted at me to go away.

So I did.

But the byre and the cows weren't far enough. It was the sea I needed. My aunt's words followed me, and the air swarmed with irritable humors. My feet pounded the path with a satisfying crunch and set gravel rattling down the cliff and onto the beach below. Collecting my stone sack from its hidey-hole, I dragged it past the rocks and to the edge of the water. Our spread of white sand and half-moon of foam made me welcome and filled me up with content.

One of the seals had chosen to whelp alone in our cove this year, though hundreds of her fellows were doing likewise just around the corner in the next cove. It was a strange thing for a seal to be so solitary. They commonly like the company of their kind and can't be persuaded away, even for fish. This lone mother lay on her side, head and tail both held off the ground, and watched me stamp past. The hungry pup at her teat stopped feeding to watch too as I, dragging my sack behind me, walked straight into the sea and raised a cloud of fussing gulls all about us. I waded into the warm water up to my waist, to my chest, to my shoulders, and when the sea reached my chin, I just took a deep breath and kept on walking.

At the last moment, I filled myself with air. I sucked it in until I felt I was mostly air and my body a ghostly thing. The sea rose over my face, and I opened and closed my eyes to accustom them to the salt. There was a rush in my ears, and all the din and heat dropped away. A few more paces and I was at the edge of the drop, where the sand stopped and fell away into dark water and the kelp forests.

Straightaway I stepped off the drop and into the dappled place. My sack was stuffed with stones and shells for ballast, and I sank to the seabed and settled cross-legged into the sand and grit. I gazed upward through giantess's ribbons of wrack and waving weed. Above me, the sun rolled over the water's surface like a silver ball and shot its cold light into the warm depths, reaching down even to where I sat, as far away from the surface as I could. Below me, the sand shifted and sea beetles wriggled up and out into the water, swimming here in the speckled world just as they fly above.

Half a furlong into the kelp forest, the water darkens and starts to drag at the weed. In some places the sea meadow is pushed flat and the whole sea seems to be rushing past. I feel the drag of it. At times it seems to want to pull me away. When that happens, I stuff more stones into my sack to stop myself sailing off like an untethered boat in a storm. Mostly, though, it's peaceful, and the best place to think.

The cove's creatures were good companions to me then, and almost as diverting as stories. This day a red crab unfolded itself inside some nearby bones and made a dash for the cover of its rocks, dragging a ragged lump of flesh behind itself like a smuggler's hoard. Its eyes, standing on their tall stalks, waggled over its shoulder as it sidled to its snug and folded itself away into the rock. There were times I'd felt that if I could become that crab or some other sort of creature, I would. I would move and talk in their simple way, eat and drink as they do without all the growing and tending and seasonal hungers. I would live among them without being insulted and told to go away. I knew this day for the first time that though they were my companions, the creatures could never be my friends. They just didn't understand.

How can a person be in between themselves? You're always just you, aren't you? It's not like there's a you here and a you there — and you're also in the middle somewhere. You can't be on the way to yourself; you're always just right where you are. Aren't you?

I don't know how long I sat in the drop, but suddenly I knew I wasn't alone. Urchins, sea horses, red crabs, and such don't trouble my solitude. Only something like me can do that: something warm-blooded and with a type of sense and loyalty. A seal can trouble me, an otter too—and other creatures that come and go but I never see up close, like whales passing on the other side of the wrack. My breath was almost gone now and I felt my body straining toward the air, but there was something there, something hidden in the kelp, and it was something human-like. I leaned forward and stared deep into the forest.

A stillness among the moving curl and tangle of wrack drew my eye. A long shadow rocked in there. Two wild, black eyes were watching me as I watched. A mottled body stretched away back into the speckled light, two tiny hands parted the kelp, and I saw the tail, sinuous, and a face. Its mouth parted in what looked like a grin, and bubbles rose from its lips and nose as if it tried to talk. Then, as quickly as it came, it turned and slipped like a ghost back into the forest of dim beams and rays.

Only a year before, I would have run to tell Auntie Ushag, but all that had changed. I didn't know any longer how to talk to her. She would only roll her eyes and tell me to go away. After all the trouble over a dream, I wasn't about to lure her jibes and temper again. My breath rushed out of me, and I emptied my sack and rose to the sun.

I can't help seeing what I see. It's in me to notice things. I don't mean to.

I sweated that summer through in the heat of my need to know everything my aunt wouldn't tell. I needled and poked and kept on until she told me I put the lie to the old saying that it's better to be quarreling than lonesome. She said that lately she envied lonely people. If she wouldn't start talking, there were others who wouldn't stop. I had an eye for them.

Monthly market days in Shipton were the only days my aunt and I mixed with the others. It was there I'd overheard the talk about us. Why would the Marreys choose to live out there in that wild and shattered place, the earwigs muttered, two women alone and far from humankind? Nothing but the sea to look upon, they told each other, slipping me pitying looks that made me want to bang their heads together. Nobody but each other . . . and the girl growing up now, they whispered, casting cold eyes upon Auntie Ushag.

Last market day of the fall, I'd overheard them in the baker's snug. That Neen Marrey looks to have grown into a sweet girl, one said, and they all made what would have been sounds of agreement, were they not all three sheets to the wind. As it was, they

sounded like a coven, cackling and spitting and slapping the table. I pressed closer into the wall shadows
to hear more. Baker's Cushie said, What she needs
is company of her own age, and Ushag should be
ashamed, hiding her away in that dark corner of the
island to rot and lose all her chances. . . . The young
one's like a shy little wood violet. The table of women
shrieked like gulls trailing the boats.

You know, she went on loudly, full of herself now
that she had them all listening. I've heard that violets
grow sweeter when grown near something bitter . . .
like onions. The onions draw to themselves the foul-
ness in the soil, see, leaving all the sweetness to the
violets. She made a vinegar mouth, and then, as if
she couldn't wait, she spat ale and almost burst. That
would explain a lot about those two, now, wouldn't it?

Their nasty whispering made me angry. They had a
neat way of tucking their point inside something soft-
seeming and neighborly. The cutting edge was hidden
in a joke or a piece of advice. It was like being sliced
by a tiny blade hidden in a goose feather; it took a
moment to realize the wound. Every market day, there
was a barb for my aunt, and one for me. We were
nothing but a type of pastime to them, and it made
me even angrier that in one thing their nasty whispers
were right. I would have given just about anything to
have a friend who wasn't a cow.

In the face of Market-Shipton, I watched my aunt clamp her mouth into its tight line and fold her scarred brown arms across her chest. She bargained hard and was fair and honest, but she tried no market friendships. She never drank with the women, and we left as soon as trade was done. Everybody thought her too proud by half and just asking for a fall, but if she heard any of the barely hidden talk, she never mentioned it.

Not me, though. I heard most things. It's in me to listen, and I don't see why I shouldn't. How do you ever find things out otherwise? I overheard Mr. Owney in the pub say that Pa was a drinker who'd killed Mam by mistake. One year, he said, a year of the Hunger, Colm plowed her under with the dead greens after putting away two bottles all by himself. She'd fainted in the bottom field, and, all unknowing, he went right over her, horses and plowshares and feet and all.

Well, he said, it was twilight, when the eyes are easily fooled. Everybody smiled. And she was always a little brown woman. Easy to miss, flat on the ground and in that light. Everybody laughed.

Then Colm Breda drowned all right. Mr. Owney sighed, shaking his head. Poor fella fell in a whiskey vat—and died trying to drink his way out! It took some time after this for their merriment to die down.

I despised them. They didn't even try to make a

good story. This one was just plain wrong; Pa drowned a whole year before Mam disappeared. Men from Merton found his boat and his woolen in the Breda weave still in mostly one piece and brought them back to us. I don't understand people sometimes. They can be dumb as dirt and crueler than any creature.

Some folk say Pa married a merrow and that, being able in the water and full of jealousy, Mam went after him and was drowned by his new wife and her minnows. They say Carrick's men have always bred with the merrows. They say that's why they live in such numbers in our waters; they all have family ashore.

Others say Mam lost her mind from the grief after Pa died. They say she walked the island without stopping, half-dressed and skeleton-like, for an entire year, and then disappeared. There are people who say they've seen her in the tunnels and caves of the cliffs; they say she's white-haired now, and perfectly pale and transparent in the body, so as you can see her heart, and it's broke clean in two. Some saw her boarding a missionary boat for the mainland, alone and pitiful.

Each story is worse than the last.

Scully Slevin is a different sort of fish, though. He was sixteen and lived with his mam over the rise of Shipton-Cronk and up the moaney. They were our closest neighbors but still a good afternoon's walk away. Of course, Ushag didn't hold with mixing. To her, friendship brought bother, so we didn't see them much, but during the last Hunger, people helped each other as they could, and Ma Slevin has never forgotten the Marreys. She speaks jewels of Mam's kindness and of my aunt's great heart. That Hunger was long past, though, and I couldn't see signs of any great heart in Ushag, as hard as I looked.

Anyway, I don't remember that Hunger. It's ancient history. It doesn't mean anything to me.

Scully's blind, and he plays his fiddle for money on market days and on all the other days for free. He plays tunes that catch you. Everybody dances as they pass Scully's jig. I once saw a man and woman stop right in the middle of a brawl and start spinning each other around. The music took the fight right out of them. Of course, he also plays tunes that drag the heart right out of your chest, but he doesn't do that so often. I don't think he's sure what to do with people's tears.

At that last fall market, just before winter set in and we all closed ourselves in against the cold, he grabbed at my hand as I passed him. Out of the blue, he told me that I should be proud to be Neen Marrey. Not only did our family have the merrow blood, but the Marreys were one of the few families left on Carrick that once had our very own banshee. He told me

I was truly lucky. He said he'd give his sight to see a banshee.

I pointed out that he'd already lost his sight, so it wasn't his to give any longer.

He tightened his old fiddle pegs and said, as if I should know better, "Not that sight."

CHAPTER TWO

Changeling

I N EARLY SUMMER I TOLD Auntie Ushag what Scully had told me at the market, about the merrows and our family, and that was the start of all our bother and quarrels. That first time, she folded her arms across her chest and looked at me for a good while before speaking. Then she sighed.

"Why are we to listen to Scully Slevin?" she asked.

"Because he's a seer," I told her simply and truthfully.

"Listen to me," she said slowly and clearly, speaking as though I were old or deaf or stupid. "Scully is not a seer. There are no seers. Those days, if they were ever here, are gone. Everybody knows that. And it's a good thing too," she added.

"Why?" I asked.

"Because those days were a mess."

"Why?"

"No one knew where they stood. All those sprites and half-beings and whatnots, they had too many rules. Don't build around the barrows, don't plant in the dancing grounds, don't fall asleep under the alder or pick the columbine from Strangers' Croft. Who could remember all that? Then they had holidays every other day! With presents and special clothes, and feast food. And wine, barrels and barrels of wine. Nobody got any work done. The Little Brothers and their one god are better." She paused. "Slightly."

I could see I had one question left before she would stop answering me, saying that my questions were becoming a conversation and she had no time to converse like a scholar or a lady or any other person with no real purpose.

I asked as quietly as I could, "Why?"

My aunt put her hand on my shoulder and looked into my eyes. "Because they're simple, Neen. Ten rules, three holidays, and one god who made everything. Simple." She turned back to the washing. "Anyway, there hasn't been a real sighting of the Others for centuries. Scully is just showing off. There are no seers anymore. No seers, no merrows, no selkies —"

I perked up. "What are selkies?"

"They're nothing." She punched and wrung the wet wool. "I've done talking. I don't have any more time to waste. Take these and spread them and leave me alone."

Up the cove, we were a house of secrets, but all I had to do was find Scully or visit down at the Slevin place to be glutted with all the stories I wanted. All through that winter, Bo and I'd been sneaking down to sit among the whelk shells, fat hens, and wood ash in Ma Slevin's smoky snug and listen as she blathered. In this manner I'd learned of the flooding, trembling, and burials that have rocked the island. In times past, the very earth has opened up and swallowed whole villages. The sun shines for a month and the lake becomes a bog; rain falls for a month and the bog becomes a lake. You never know with earth and water what's going to happen next, Scully says, almost cheerfully. Out in the cove, there's even an island that appears and disappears as it will.

At other times the sea has risen up in waves that drowned the low-lyingest, edge-most parts of the island, with the result that on clear mornings, fishermen out in the calm cove can see those undersea forests of leafless elm and alder still standing. Not only that, but they see the old paths cutting through the old forest's wavering shadows. At night, lights glint and flicker along these deep paths, and Ma Slevin says they're the souls of the poor drowned cottagers searching for one another and for a way back into the sun. The manner of their dying is leeching them of human warmth, she told us, and they are well on their way to becoming cold-blooded water sprites. They live an icy, lonely existence, forever searching for something they dimly recall as "companionship" and for a way back to a fading memory of something called "home." Ma has a way of putting things that makes pictures in my head.

Sometimes the waves only wash everything away— old landforms and new monasteries and all—and then retreat with their hoard to deep water. At the bottom of the top lake on a clear, bright night, you can see the steeple of a drowned church. Those who have the ears to hear, Ma Slevin whispered to us, can still hear the bells toll of a Sunday morning. God Be Praised for His Good Bells, she added, crossing herself. It's a beautiful thing, and lucky they are who hear it.

During that long, wet winter, they told me, too, of our last brownie. He still lives down at the barrows, where the Old ones used to store grain and weapons, but being the only one of his kind left has shaped him into a secretive, bile-ridden creature. He no longer helps with household work or dances outside at weddings but just squats in his barrow, now sleeping, now grumbling, and always stinking like a pit.

I felt sorrowful for that lonely brownie. I think it must be hard to be the only one of something. Scully says it's not that bad, and he should know. He walks alone except for his old fiddle, and he never stumbles. His head and eyes roll as he goes, but each footfall is steady. He stops often to feel the sun on his face and takes slow high-steps like a cricket in the summer grass. Sometimes I close my eyes and try to walk like Scully. When you walk blind, arriving anywhere seems a victory of some kind. Even more than a victory; it seems like a miracle. Most of the time, I just fall over.

Ma's place draws creatures to it. Auntie Ushag has dug out most of the flowers from our gardens to encourage the bees into the meadows behind us, closest to the hives, but Ma's garden is full of bees feeding all anyhow. Birds come for the unswept crumbs and then nest all around the house, including one pair of stubborn eaves warblers right over the door. They shit on the threshold, but instead of chasing them off, Ma just throws water over the mess, shouting as she does so to warn any passing ghosts to whom the wet would be worse than fire. Hedge pigs come for the milk that she puts out in dishes for them. She says she has no choice; if she didn't, the hedge pigs would take it directly, and that's a terrible shock for any cow. They nearly die of shame.

I watched Scully move around his place, steady and

sure. He cooked. He tended the fire. He never spilled anything. He never burned himself. He couldn't see, and his mam was too old and stiff to care, so the mess of shells and fish bones we were building around the hearth just grew taller and wider around us as outside the winter sleet flew and the black clouds crowded in. I loved their place.

While Ma told the stories, Scully added the detail. He knew a lot about the Others that even his mam didn't. For instance, he knew that faery talk is not pretty like tinkling bells at all. It's a lumpy sort of language, and everything they say in it sounds like a declaration of war. But they can, and will, take away wounds or deformities if they are asked decently.

"Well, why don't you ask for Scully's sight?" I asked Ma, convinced that if anyone could persuade a faery, that person would be Ma herself, with all her trust and good nature. She smiled fondly on her son and said, "Ah, now. There's a pert question. Will you be requiring your eyesight anytime, Scully?"

"No, Ma, and thank you very much," he answered. He thought for a moment and added, "It could be seen as mighty ungrateful."

Ma nodded. "That's right, my Birdie," she said. "Would you rather see the world, or see beyond it?" Scully blew his nose. I looked at my feet. I felt a long story coming on, and I stoked the fire, then settled into Bo's warm hide to hear it. She lowed to me in a friendly manner, and Scully shushed her.

"It's said that it's a wise father who knows his own child," Ma began, "but there's times when the same may be said about a mother.

"When I was young, I was married to a peat man and sent out here to the moaney to live with him. The bog was drier then, and less stenching. He was a good man, and we were happy for many, many years before it all went wrong. It took years before I conceived of a child, and when it finally happened, I went about singing for weeks on the strength of it. (It always seems a shining miracle, in spite of it being the most ordinary thing in the world.) There was still a rash of sickness about after the last Hunger, but I was well and the baby kicked me strong enough, so I had no bother or worries.

"I remember that spring well." She sighed, and her nose ran.

"The babe arrived, and he was a big, bonny boy. He already had a full head of hair, and his father nearly busted his jaw smiling as he held his son for the first time, and he said, 'Look at that arm, Mureal. He's already mighty . . . mighty like a Christian!' We were about as pride-puffed as two new parents can be, feeling as how we were the only ones to ever do this thing, and how our boy was the beautifulest baby ever born, and other such sinful thinking.

"Well, we were punished for it. One morning I go to his cradle to feed him, and he's gone. In his place is this shriveled, wailing thing, looking more like a stick than a babe. Its arms and legs are twigs, and its face withered and covered in bark rings. As soon as it sees me, it starts up shrieking, and it doesn't stop. I knew at once what it was.

"It was a changeling. Having heard of the birth of a fat, healthy mortal baby, the Others had come in the night and taken our boy. It's a simple truth and well-known fact that their babies are thin and ugly and they're jealous of us human mothers.

"It being generally agreed that the old days were gone and the Other Ones vanished, if they'd ever been at all, we couldn't find any help. The charmers all remain silent these days. You can't find a body to remove a curse or eat a sin anymore, not even for real coins. I searched and asked all about the markets and public houses, but nobody listened. I went to the Little Brothers; they were kind and told me to pray to Jesus, but I could tell they didn't believe me.

"At last, a so-called friend told me that in the villages pity for my loss was running thin and I'd best stop spreading stories and hunting charmers before folk ran out of patience completely. She looked at the unnatural lump in the cradle and declared it human but sickly. A mother knows, though. A mother knows.

"That awful offspring I found in the cradle that morning didn't live. I stopped feeding it, and it soon perished. We had to bury it in the churchyard despite knowing its Otherwise origins. It was terrible to hear the poor Father praying over that ungodly lump and see the waste of the holy water and suchlike. Everyone thought it was grief made me so white and jumpy, but it was fear. I expected their Christian grave to spit the body back up at every moment of that service."

Ma stopped to blow her nose and to spit. She lit her pipe and stared into the flames for a long while. I waited. I didn't want to talk in case she stopped. I'd never been so happy. Ushag and I were warm and safe at home; we were content in our company as animals in their den are, we were soothed by the breath and body of each other, cozy in the smells and the sounds of home, and content in our work, but however comfortable I was at home, I missed something. It was something I couldn't grasp, something nameless and shapeless but so real I could feel the hole inside me where it would fit. Here, by Ma's messy fireplace, I could feel that place filling a little.

"Well, that was that," Ma went on, "and Pherick and I gave up our quest to find that first boy. I won't say we got over it, but folk have ever lost children and there's nothing to be done about it, though I envied mothers and fathers whose children had simply died. As is its habit, life went on, and within a month of the burial, I was expecting again, and we poured our hope into this coming child.

"Our second was again a beautiful child. This time a daughter, with ears like pink shells and a good, strong shout on her! We enjoyed her for a month, hidden in our home and giving the news to no one. I slept her next to my bed to make sure.

"But there was no escaping it. One night I went to bed, and when I woke she had followed her brother. The Others had come and silently taken her from my very side. This time the impostor seemed more human, but it didn't fool me. This red-faced monster with its rolling eyes wasn't my daughter. As I said, a mother knows her child.

"This time I didn't try to find help. There was no point. I just had to let her go, and that time was the worst of my life. Pherick didn't speak for weeks and spent most of his time out in the cove. I only went to the village for the market and didn't stay to chat. I was changed by it all, and entirely done in. That was when I stopped visiting down there, and met your mam and Ushag. Ven used to come up and sit with me." Ma stopped and looked at me with her bleary eyes. "She could sit like nobody I've known. Quiet and calm as a warm bath.

"It was her as told me what people used to do about changelings in the old days. It was of no interest to me anymore, as I'd decided never to have another child, but it was a comfort to have someone even pretend to believe me. As it turned out, she was right, and I have every good reason to be thankful to her.

"In spite of deciding to remain childless, I was expecting again within the year. I spent my time fretting and picking at my food, and Pherick spent his fixing locks and bolts, and sharpening his blades. I told him that if the Others wanted to come in, locks and bolts wouldn't stop them, and he told me that's all I knew, for the Other Ones were done in by iron. His preparations put the heart back into him, and I couldn't bring myself to take that away from him, but I knew we were as doomed in this next babe as in the other two. Flying in the face of nature, I grew thinner as I neared my time.

"And then Scully was born. He wasn't a fat, healthy baby like the others, but he was quiet and sweet, and he fed well, so I had my hopes. I thought maybe the Others wouldn't want this one, as he wasn't their usual type, but I was wrong. They came in the second month.

"I woke one day and there he was. Gone."

I looked at Scully. He had his face turned to the fire

and the shadows playing there hid his expression. His fingers moved on his knees like pale spiders.

"They'd come through the rat holes and left a white twig in Scully's place, like it wasn't even worth cutting a proper log for him. This time I sat by the twig as it wailed, and for days I prayed. I prayed to the Little Brothers' god (who was likely to know what it is to have a son in trouble), in spite of knowing the Others to be godless and therefore unlikely to be under Christian orders. I prayed to the saints, them having more freedom of movement, as it were, than Himself, who plainly can't be seen to be mixing with the Other sort. I prayed to Breeshey and the Good Mother Mary and to the Nameless One Herself, and all the rest. In the middle of all the praying, I fell asleep.

"I must have dreamed a memory of Ven's stories, because I was all at once awake in the night and I knew what to do. I picked up that wailing twig. It looked at me with knowing, watchful eyes, and it said to me, 'What art thou doing, Mammy?' and then I threw it in the fire. There was one terrible cry, the fire blazed out of the hearth, and I fell senseless.

"When I woke in the morning, Scully was back and hungry. We never saw the Others again. But there was one thing I hadn't considered.

"It's a simple fact that Other time is different from ours. In the three days he'd been gone from our world, in the Otherworld, he'd lived seven years and was almost a grown-up. He'd lived with his Other mother and learned their Other ways for all that time, but he returned to us as he'd been when they took him; he came back a baby. And we were strangers to him! It took time for him to settle. Having to repeat his first seven years over made him bad-tempered for a while, and he'll always be a bit Otherwise — but praise be to God, it's a beautiful thing, and comes in useful too.

"Of course, he did come back to us blinded; the great blaze of the Otherworld Halls being too much for his poor eyes. The Others never take something without leaving something else in its stead, though, and they gave him the Othersight to make up for it. He looks upon a different world from us, and sees us in ways we can never see ourselves." Ma stood, stretching her stiff back and placing her spotted hand on his head. She moved to the corner of the darkening cottage and lit a taper. By its light, among a heap of stones and shells, I saw the Christian's cross and a fresh green alder branch, a set of antlers, a stone spiral, and a bowl of milk, all set in the niche behind her bed. She gave each one a touch or a kiss, whispering and blowing and moving her hands in spirals. She drew a woman-sized circle in the air and stepped through it. "All that talking's thirsty work. Who's for a brew, then?" she asked briskly. Then she bent to me and whispered, "By the way, never trust a salamander. Nasty, feverish things!"

Scully turned his face to me, and his eyes looked straight into mine, milky in the candlelight and amused.

"My mother leaves nothing to chance," he said. "And that's a simple fact."

CHAPTER THREE

Roundhouse

S TOP LOOKING AT ME LIKE THAT!" Auntie
Ushag slopped the rag around in the bowl, spilling
both water and wort into the dust of our yard. "What
a face," she muttered.

I lowered my eyes and watched the drops drying in
the heat as she turned her back to me and remixed the
cure. Dust and leaves rose in tiny spirals and settled
again without a sign of having moved. I didn't dare
look up. We had a plague of irritableness in the yard.

Looking away toward the cliff, I tried to arrange
my face. I didn't know what she meant by things like
that. I tried out a little smile, but I could feel it dying
before I could lift my head. I tried widening my eyes
in a show of interestedness, but my aunt just took
one look at me and sighed. Behind me, Bo skittered
around the yard, pushing her nose into everything,
eventually pushing her head under my arm and licking

my face with her rough, milky tongue. I was thankful to have something friendly to look at. Ushag wrung out the rag and pressed the cure to my skin. Bo licked at that too, but my aunt slapped her on the shoulder and said in a piercing way, "Wheesh! Gerchaaa!" and Bo scarpered.

Summer had brought on my Scale. It starts with a Heat, followed by a Prickle, and then the Reddening sets in. My forearms often look like sizable redfish when it comes on, and this time I'd been scratching so hard as to bring blood. Ushag said I was too old to be so weak-willed, but still she tended me, as she always has. My aunt has a gift for such things, and an uncommon sickness or rash was then the only thing that could make her smile.

This Scale has always been somewhat of a mystery, at first being put down to an overheating of my already warm humors, and then to an overabundance of fish in my diet, and finally to an unhealthy attachment to the sea in my mother. The cures have been many, and none have yet rid me of it. I've been rubbed daily with boiled pearlwort, which turns to a disgusting sort of jelly, and fed for months on nothing but pig meat and clover, but the worst cure was being kept from the sea. Ushag said I needed to clear my mind of salt and scales, and maybe my skin would clear too.

So for a week last summer, my aunt gave me work

only around the house and yard, and up at the hives and orchard, and I was an exile from the cove. It had always been my nature to be easy, so I did as she said, but my heart wasn't in it.

I dragged myself around the house for a week with my body leaking its liveliness and the world growing greyer with each day. I sorted the skins, saving only those that were still whole enough to work. Decayed herbs, corrupted salt fish and meat, and rotted bottom-of-the-basket apples and onions were all I knew for seven days as I sorted out our stores. There were roots growing through the roof, and dangling into the hanging meats, that needed trimming. I had nightmares of damp rags and buckets, and I daydreamed of being allowed to collect even stinking weed and razor shells again if it meant I could go to the shore.

All the bleached timber and rusted bolts we'd hoarded from the beach, where bad weather always lands us useful goods, were finally put to use. Some of it had been sitting there from the time before my birth. We patched and rebuilt some of the wall around the door. We made a new stall in the cow byre for Bo. We even built me a new bed, as I'd grown too long for the other one. Finally we sewed together the rabbit-and-hare skins I'd saved from ruin and made a fine winter rug.

At last, our newly swept and washed house was

done. I'd never been anywhere so clean. Ushag and I stood among the baskets of sweet apples and crisp onions, and looked into the smoky roof where hung all that fresh green kale, the sharp herbs, and hooks of dried fish—and we were both silenced, entirely. It was unsettling, almost unnatural.

It was stranger still because, I discovered that week, my aunt had a secret. Over the years she had gathered not only useful but beautiful things from the wreckage that turned up on our beach. The trunk that held it all sat in its dark corner, and we stacked firewood on it. During that great house scouring, from curiosity I prised it open. It held heavy, stitched fabrics that we could have hung at wind-rise to keep the warm inside. There were shining metal platters and jugs we could have eaten from instead of our ordinary trenchers. There were gold hoops such as some women in the towns wear in their ears. There were even two twisting silver candlesticks, but we never used any of it. My aunt had never mentioned the trunk.

Staying away from the sea for a week didn't help my skin. The Scale neither spread nor did it go away. At night I lay awake and listened miserably for the waves, and all day I sniffed sadly at the salty air while I worked, until finally Ushag couldn't bear me any longer. One morning, one early morning of sunbeams and motes, she just said "Go!" and I went before she could change her mind. My Scale is just a part of me now, and we live with it.

It took weeks for the house to regain its homely air once more, and neither of us slept well again until it did. A strange smell of nothing comes off such cleanness, and it freezes up the nose and throat. I sneezed for days. Who knows what unhealthy humors rise in all that emptiness and shine? At last, though it took the whole winter, we were settled back into chaff dust and pollen once more.

Ushag now put the cloth to my arm, and I had to look somewhere, anywhere but at her, so I watched as the cure ran over my peeling skin and back into the bowl. I watched closely at first to head off my aunt from being irritated by my face and to make her think I was interested in the cure, but then because another notion occurred to me. When I looked closely and really saw it, the fact is that Scale of mine could be scales.

Real scales.

Fish scales.

They looked just like them.

They could be the outward sign of my true self, I thought while studying them. They could be a sign from my blood, the Marrey blood writing itself on the pages of my skin. I didn't know if such things were possible, but I supposed that if my aunt were able to read a look on my face I didn't even know I had, then there could easily be other secrets inside a person's body. It didn't seem any less likely than murders or madness, or running away from your own child just because a husband dies.

When I first conceived the thought, I felt as I do on the dawn sand, its crust perfect, before I take the first step of a brand-new day. I felt as though suddenly my life made sense; all the motley stories about my mother, the sea, and me formed into a perfect circle. Without thinking, I raised my eyes to my aunt's, and straightaway she saw my face and the new thing in it; she said, "What?"

"In town they say Pa married a merrow," I said as simply as I could. I didn't ask her if it was true; I just said it, and quietly too. I wanted her to talk to me, and she wouldn't if I seemed to be questioning her.

"I know." She squeezed the compress, and we both watched the cure flow. "They mean he drowned."

"They say that Mam went after him."

"I know that too." She lifted my arm and picked at the tough red skin. It didn't really hurt; it just felt tender. "They mean they don't know what happened to her."

I felt myself grow hot. "Well, why don't they say what they mean, then?"

My aunt shook her head. "That I don't know.

Maybe they just enjoy telling stories." She wrapped my whole arm in a cloth. "Maybe it makes the hard things easier."

I suddenly wanted Ushag to tell me, as she did when I was little, that our family had a simple story. I wanted her to tell me that we were ordinary people and, like it or not, ordinary people were born and had children and died. They came and they went away. I wanted her to tell me, and I wanted to believe her again.

"Tell me." I picked at my hands and peeled off one perfect scale. I held it up in the light, a tiny silver flake.

"You're getting too big for all this." My aunt crossed her arms and looked at me. "I've told you a hundred times."

"One more time." If it hadn't been for the Scale, I don't think she'd have given in. As it was, she was distracted by tending it and began to speak. Her sing-song tone told me she would tell it and tell it all, as she used to.

"It's a simple fact that Colm Breda died strong and dutiful while fishing in his own waters from his own boat. There's many worse ways of dying. What of those who die alone in strange seas? Or those bound by barbarians and heathens and burned far from home? What of those hanged, or made to swallow poison, or worse?"

I'd never been able to imagine what might be

worse, but my aunt's list of these possible ways to die somehow managed to make my own father's death seem a reasonable, almost pleasant thing.

"People, still living and known to be decent, truthful folk, found his coracle washed up by Strangers' Croft, empty of line and bait and man. His woolen had washed up at Merton and we recognized it by its pattern of Breda coils and knots, which is the usual manner we know any of the drowned. Faces are the first to be eaten in the sea.

"Not uncommon," said Ushag. "Not very exciting. That's how life can be, and usually is for most of us. Your father was not a hero or a legend. He was a fisherman and he died by the sea. It was all as it should have been." She stopped talking and placed my hands in the bowl. She was silent for such a time that I thought she'd finished.

"And Mam?" I prompted her.

"Again?" she said.

I nodded.

"This is the last time," my aunt told me. "I don't want to talk about it again after this." She raised her eyebrows at me. I nodded. She dropped her eyes and began talking again. Her words ran together, and the singsong tone flattened.

"My sister married for love. He was the youngest of the Breda boys from out at Merton, and he came to live out here with us after they wed. The Bredas had plenty of sons, but us Marreys had been all girls, six in my generation. We lost two sisters before they were weaned, one more to a Hunger and one to the traveling nuns. By the time Ven married Colm and brought him home, there was only our father and her and me left."

I did something I'd never done—I interrupted the story.

"What was she like?" I asked.

"She was nearly sixteen." Ushag gave me a stony look. "I was nearly twelve. Within a few months, my father died and you were born. We four were happy together.

"Then one day your pa went out after pout and dab, and he didn't come back. At first, Ven waited, day after day and all day, at the harbor, but Colm never came. After a few weeks, she took to sleeping day after day, all day, and took against talking. She wouldn't listen to anyone. She just slept and shrank to a twig.

"After they fetched his woolen to her and there was no pretending left, she took to taking her misery out walking. She walked it for whole days, only coming in at dark. Then days and nights would pass. They even saw her in the south, all over Shipton-Cronk and up the moaney and even around Strangers' Croft. Scully's ma was always bringing her home. She used to turn up at their place, and they'd let her just sit inside until she'd done. It was kind of them."

I was excited to be able to offer something more to the story. "She helped during Ma's troubles," I said.

"What troubles would they be?" Ushag dried my hands and smeared them in red fishy jelly.

"The Others took all her children and only Scully came back but he came back blind from what he'd seen there and Themselves gave him the Othersight to make up for it and Ma says he sees things we don't, and Ma said Mam could just sit quiet like no one she's ever known," I said in a rush, and then asked again, "What was she like?" I asked like it was nothing to me if I got an answer or not.

"Well, she didn't just sit here with us, did she? Not through our troubles." My aunt began folding up her rags and boxing the roots and bark and suchlike. Her face was such as I couldn't read it, but the nose on her seemed to have been sharpened, and her lips were a line as she went on with her story.

"One day your mother just kept walking and she never came home again. I don't know where she went, but she left the island. She must have, because she's not here, is she?

"Your mother just left out of a broken heart," she told me. "Sometimes it's like that. She left because she couldn't stay. You were nearly three. She was nearly nineteen. I was nearly fifteen. And that was that."

All those years stretched away behind us, but I couldn't remember them. Once, there had been the four of us in the roundhouse and yard. Now there were two, and only one of us knew how it had happened.

With everybody gone, Auntie Ushag had taken over managing the place all by herself. She learned its plots and orchard, its smoking and salting, and its dairy, and she never let the fire in the hearth die. She taught me well. We worked together at first, and when I was ready, I did it alone. We fished the cove, and we foraged and gathered along the shore and in the woods. We grew greens and tended to the herbs and honey that grow wild all around us. Eventually, we bartered enough to achieve a cow, and Breck came to the yard. Then Breck was covered and she had Bo, and here we were; four of us again.

My aunt never complained, though she had reason sometimes, and she rarely smiled, though she had reason for that too. She never said I should be grateful. Which was good, because I wasn't. This day I could smell the lies off Auntie Ushag as strong as wild garlic. My face hardened against her, and she put her hands on her hips and gazed up into the sky. I felt a longing to poke her.

"Mam might come home." I watched my aunt closely. "You don't really know where she went. You said so yourself."

"No, but I'm sure it wasn't to the merrows and water sprites, Neen." Ushag was cold-voiced and ugly with it. She only dragged my name out to scorn me. "I wish she would come back. It's all very well for her."

"What does that mean?" I asked.

"It means I'm it for you, and I wish you'd stop it. Ven is gone, and I am still here. Just leave it be."

I watched her as she gathered together the rags and bark and leaves into their box, and emptied the bowl over the wall. She seemed sharpened into all elbows, knees, and other bones. There didn't seem to be any warm flesh to her anymore. She was like bones under a slim, rough cover. Without even looking at me, she snapped again, "Stop looking at me like that," and went toward the house.

As she passed, she whispered, "She was just like you."

CHAPTER FOUR

Merrow

MY OWN SNEEZING WOKE ME LATE. Too hot even to lie there napping until Ushag came to rouse me, and I sat up and leaned back onto the cool stone wall. In the glare beyond our front door, a hen was taking its dust bath, wings outspread and body rising and settling. I closed my eyes and listened.

Nothing. Only the hens and their drawn-out, hot-day calls that sound like cows, which a baffled Bo sometimes answers. No wind. No cloud. It was to be another blue day, another day when the sky ate everything. I would need to find shade. The beach is too bright on these days. I forced myself up and out. As I passed into the blaze, something small and dark fell at my feet. I bent to see. It was an eaves warbler, still breathing but senseless. I pushed it into the wall shadow with my toes.

I shuffled close-eyed to the cow byre, where straightaway my aunt was face-to-face with me.

"The birds are fainting," I told her. To anyone else it would've been the opening of a conversation, but not my aunt.

"Up at last," was what she said. In her wide-brimmed basket hat and long shift, I thought she looked like a mushroom. I picked up the bucket and drank, the milk coating my mouth and only setting up another sort of thirst.

"You look like a mushroom." With surprise, I heard myself saying it out loud. It was like I was somebody else speaking.

Auntie Ushag made a show of ignoring me, but I knew she'd heard. She leaned against the door, watching me. "And you look like a girl who needs a job," she said as I buried my face in Bo's neck. "I know. I have just the thing for such a day. You should go up the woods." I shrugged. She threw the bucket to me, and I was forced to catch it. "We need honey," she said, and added, sugar sweet, "Don't get sticky."

Ma told me a story about the Little Brothers' hell once, but it had too much hitting and burning for my taste. I like stories with a mystery and some comical talk. Also, their hell seemed nothing to do with me.

My hell is the sort of place in which everything is always faintly sticky. It moves with you, traveling from everything to your fingers, to your hands, and from there to your face and neck, even to your hair, until every part of you and of the place is sticky. Moving it from place to place, part to part, doesn't diminish the stickiness one jot. Getting honey from wild bees is like that. You find it between your fingers days later, in your ears, and once I found it between my toes. There's always more of it to spread around. My aunt walked backward into the sunlight, smirking. She knew very well about my hell.

I dunked myself headfirst in the water barrel and stuffed fistfuls of almonds and hazels and yellow cheese into my bag. My head was full of the things I would've liked to say to Ushag, and my heart grumbled darkly. The only brightness lay in the promise of the cool shade of the grove of bees.

I dragged my feet through the dry yard, past my aunt stooping among the wilting greens, and beyond the wall with its vines and lizards. I didn't take my hat, and I knew she saw that I didn't. I also didn't take a cover for the bucket, or my net and gloves. Bitterness was in my belly, like nettles. Beyond the orchard, our cropping trees give way to alder, elm, ash, and rowan, to hawthorn and pine, and toadstools in fall. Scully's ma would have it that every mound, tree, and pond in the wild groves is an opening to the Otherworld, and every clearing one of their feasting places. I looked but just saw sunlight among the green leaves, and hard black shadows on the ground.

All my body was impatient. There was a life being made for me somewhere, and all I had to do was get there. The path ahead wavered like water as I rushed and clattered along it. Then I heard music.

It was just Scully. His fiddle has its own scratchy voice. It doesn't sound like anything but itself. I snuck up on him to see. He was leaning against a hawthorn with his tune sobbing and hiccoughing all around him. At once, my eyes filled with the tears they carried. He stopped playing.

"Neen Marrey!" he said, smiling into the air. "Weren't you taught it's rude to eavesdrop?" He laid his fiddle on the grass. "What are you doing up here?"

I came out from behind the tree and waved the bucket at him. Then I remembered he couldn't see it.

"Honey," I told him. "What tune was that?"

"Not sure as yet. Perhaps I'll call it after this place. What about 'Go Tell the Bees'?" He stood up. "I'll help you," he said, and reached out his hand. "Net?"

"I forgot them." I laughed. "Accidentally-on-purpose. It was stupid."

Scully didn't laugh. "Well," he said, leaning toward my voice, "we'll just have to sing sweetly to them . . . and put them under a chant."

I confess to wanting to see him do that, and to believing he could. I leaned forward and waited.

"You know, you must always come up here and tell the bees your family's news: when somebody's born or wed, and particularly if they die.

"If you don't, they'll up and leave your hives," he said.

"They're not our hives." I gave him the bucket.

"Yes, they are." He sounded surprised. "They've been Marrey bees for generations." His voice grew high and soft. "Don't let their old king hear you say that. They're easily offended." He moved toward a hive built low into an old stump where the bees were busy in the heat, and he spoke to them in his whispering singsong. I was silent. "Now, then. Listen to meee. Youse bees sing bee-ooo-ti-fully. All that hummming is the very thing, but where are the words? A song needs words."

I swear I heard the buzzing in the grove grow stronger. Scully began to sing to the bees. I couldn't hear his words, but as he sang, he stuck his hand into their hollow and felt all around for the honeycomb. I had expected him to charm the bees straightaway into just giving up their honey to us, perhaps bringing it out in little buckets and tipping it into my big one—but all he did was jump back with a yell, holding on to his dripping hand and biting his lip.

"Well," I said. "Aren't you just the wild and mystic man, now?" He was shaking his hand and cursing. "A real chanter of beasts." I looked around and saw what I was looking for. "Wrap this around it." I handed him the ribwort, and he sat down, clutching it in his wounded palm. "I would've thought you'd have seen that coming. What with the Othersight and everything."

He rolled his eyes and smiled broadly, showing all his teeth. I looked at him closely. He didn't have any shyness at all; there was no part of him that was hidden. He just grinned into the air like there was nothing to be troubled about.

His eyes were like the sea in one of its foaming humors. I leaned forward to look more closely, and he said, "Heishan, who raised you? Didn't your aunt teach you it's rude to stare?"

"What else am I going to do with you?" I told him, backing off. "It's not like we can stare at things together. How's your hand now?"

"Better." He had dropped most of the ribwort. I took his hand. It was red and swollen. He thought for a moment. "Well, it's a day for going slugabout in shady parts, isn't it? I could tell you the story of your ancestor Doolish Marrey and the merrow wife."

Right then, I would've given my own hand to the

bees to carry off to hear the real story of my merrow grandmother.

"Oh, all right, I might as well," is all I said, though. I didn't like folk knowing my deepest feelings. They were mine, and people's feelings are even more personal than their bodies. "Wrap your hand again first." I handed him fresh wort and some parsley too. "Talking will stop you interfering with my work."

He lay down on the grass and closed his eyes. "Well, if you're not interested, a nap will stop me doing that just as well."

I pushed him until he rolled over on his face. "Tell me, then," I said. He snored into the grass. "Tell me."

"All right." He rolled over, opened his eyes, and raised them to the treetops. The honeybees droned in the hawthorn grove, wood shadows moved upon his face, and slowly, the quiet fell around us. And Scully spoke. He was different. Like he knew things.

"There is a world under the waves where the people live in houses of shell, bone, and coral held together by spit. The beds are giant clams that close at night, protecting the sleepers from the shock eel and the shark. The people of that world are the merrows, and they come in both types: male and female, just as we do. They are born, they grow, and they grow old and then they die. In these ways they resemble us, and you may think this gives them a fellow feeling for mortals. It is not so.

"Our world is like a dream to them, as theirs is to us. Our ships are just so much floating wood and iron, and our men as beasts or ghosts. They watch us as we watch the bees or the clouds. They don't sing to draw sailors to themselves but only to sing, as we do. And their singing is not beautiful, at least not in any mortal way. When you hear it, lonely and proud and more real in your ears than your own voice, though, it drags you toward itself. It finds caves in your body and fills them with its wild calls.

"Whales are more real to them, and congers more their kind. They swim with all the creatures of the cold depths, and they run herds and schools for their meat. A sealskin cloak is their only cover. Both types of merrow are mottled and scaled, each to the pattern of their family, and they are fatter than in our stories, to keep the chill out. They light themselves in the pitchy deep with glowing stripes along their sides, or lanterns growing from their brows, and grow meadows of glimmer weed around their houses.

"The men of that undersea place are of unimaginable and legendary ugliness. They are small next to their women and covered in rough and disordered scales. Their arms are fin-like, and their black eye pits are set in an enormous bald head, knobbled all over like a wild pig, of which they are uncommonly proud. Those with the hugest, knobbliest domes adorn them with gardens of starfish and glass eels and suchlike—in fact, their king has a crown of pearly sea dragons, all alive and grazing on his head, upon which he plants small, sweet grasses. He goes nowhere without an undergardener or two.

"They do have long tails like their females, but it's not a tail split like a fish. It's more serpent-like, more like an eel. They swim by wig-wagging it side to side, and what with their great webbed hands and feet, a merrow man can cut through the water like a blade. Add to this rigmarole the green teeth, the weedy earholes, and the reek of the low tide—well, you can imagine.

"Their females are human-like from the waist up, but they have a fish's split tail, and their ears hang in webbed curtains around their shoulders. Not that you'd notice, as they always have hair down to their middles at least, and it grows like sea grass, thick and waving and the color of almond buds. They are webbed at the fingers with something between silk and skin. Their eyes are changeable, and they smell of good, fresh things like salmon or salt. All this changes if they ever come ashore for good, though. The green hair turns yellow in the sun, the sea-mist eyes blacken, and the silver tail slowly turns into a pair of very wide, very flat feet.

"Some of those merrows wind up matched to mortal men, but it's never through love, in spite of men's tales about it. It's always a story of theft and deception, and I'll tell you why. The secret is, if a man can but steal and hide her sealskin cloak, the poor slippery thing can never go home again. She can't descend without the cloak, and she will agree to stay with you if she thinks there's any chance of getting it back." Scully looked sad. "They know as much about a lie as a fish." Then he laughed. "Then they come ashore and begin to change. Their mortal husbands are always gutted by the loss of all that Otherworldly beauty. It turns out not very pretty, after all, to steal affection from a free creature." He turned his head to me, and his voice softened.

"But this is where the story becomes yours.

"Your great-great-grandfather Doolish, in the time of the Great Hunger, was one of the Marreys of Merton, when it was a much smaller place and in the manner of the ancient freeholds. They had a small portion just outside of the settlement, and this, along with the sea, had to feed all ten of them; that is, until three died. Then it still had to feed seven. None of the young Marreys could think of marrying until the Hunger was done, for their parents needed them to work the plots and to churn and brew and bake — and to fish.

"It is said a more brawling, scrawny, goat-footed lot weren't to be found even in the anteroom to the Christian's hell. The girls were all besoms, and the boys were scarecrows with grog blossoms. It's remarkable how the starving still manage to find drink!" Scully lowered his head for a moment. "I'm sorry for the shame of it to you."

I felt shame that I hadn't been bothered. "That's all right," I said, and tried to feel disapproving.

"Well . . ." he carried on. "At that time the Marreys were at a very low ebb. Maybe that should give us a soft heart for Doolish himself, and what he did. He must have been a lonely and desperate man by then, turning twenty-six as he was and unwifed, and it unlikely as fish breath that any mortal woman would have him.

"During the Great Hunger of the great-great-grandparents' time, the men had taken to fishing farther offshore, or to following the shoals and schools all around Carrick. Doolish had taken to sailing north and spending days and nights among the rocks, living on grog and limpets, and scouring the shore for wrecked goods, but all he found was more grog smuggled into the caves for the Little Brothers.

"He spent a week out there, fishing and drinking and singing at the moon.

"On this particular day, Doolish had been at sea for hours and was full of bubbles and heavings himself, when he saw something sizable and silver flashing in the sun ahead of him. As he breasted the high point of the swell, he discerned a stand of low rocks in the green water and, among them, curling back into his view, a huge fish tail.

"Not knowing whether the tail was still alive or dead, he approached the rocks from behind. He anchored the boat. He crept up the rocks, which hid the main body of the fish, and no doubt spent some time anticipating the feast, and the goodwill, to come. What he found was not to bring him either of those things.

"He knew at once what it was. On the tall, barnacle-crusted rock, with her back to him, sat a merrow. Wild-eyed and long-eared, she sat combing her green hair, and the gleaming, silver tail curved with grace around the base of the rock. She didn't notice him at all, and instantly he wanted her for his own. Her skin seemed to him as the palest of anemones, and the tiny crabs in her hair were to him the luckiest creatures on earth.

"Behind her, in a gap of the rock, was her spotted sealskin cloak. It was within easy reach, and from all the stories, Doolish knew just what to do. At the very moment his mortal hand touched the cloak, the merrow turned. Her eyes were as twin looking glasses brimming with slatey seas. She gazed at him indifferently for a moment, as though he were an interesting beetle. Then the sun came out, the sea shone blue, and her eyes also. It was as though she was filled with the sea's humors.

"She looked right through him with deep disinterest. Doolish backed away, holding the sealskin behind his back. Step-by-step, he closed in on his rocking boat. His heart hammered under his ribs, and his mouth was dry, not because he was frighted (merrows are smaller than mortal women and have no magic powers; all they do is natural to them), but because he was excited by what was to happen next.

"Back at home, he hid the sealskin inside the wall and sat back to wait. He had a small grog. The sun began to set. He had another small grog. His insides and his nose began to glow. Then there came a scratchy tap at the door.

"He opened it. The merrow was on the threshold, weeping. Her soft new feet were bleeding. 'Give it back to me,' she said, and her voice was deep and mournful.

"But Doolish Marrey told her that he'd doted on her from the first moment he'd laid eyes on her, and he wasn't going to give her sealskin back, because she would go away, and if she went away, he would die a broken man. He said she might as well agree to wed with him, as she couldn't go home without her sealskin anyway, and after a time, if she was good to him, he would give it back and she could go on a visit. He told her he just wanted her to stay so he could pet her and make her happy. She made him promise to honor his word, and she moved into the Marrey house. Over the following weeks, the men of Merton made excuses to drop in as often as they could, and all were envious of that lucky dog, Doolish Marrey.

"As the months passed, though, the merrow's eyes darkened to the colors of the earth: clay, loam, stone, and finally the black of the blackest peat. By the time they were wed, in the Old way, for no decent merrow would enter a church, her ears had shrunk, her hair grown yellow, and her feet, flat. As the next year passed, she forgot who she had been and grew into the quiet and hardworking wife of Doolish Marrey. They had seven offspring, and to the four that survived being born, she was a loving and careful mother.

"Of course, Doolish quickly grew unhappy in his merrow wife. She had forgotten entirely her own marvelous self and grown as ordinary as mortal women. In the south, men now ignored her and the women started to cut her for her dumb obedience to Doolish, which put them on the spot with their own husbands, and for not attending their church or their potlucks. She'd lost herself and found nothing but spite.

"As evening changes into night, and night becomes morning, however, her sea blood flowed into their offspring. Her children displayed Otherworldly tics that,

bees, and carefully replaced the bung. The honeycomb leaked golden and sweet into my bucket. I watched it flowing.

"All right?" asked Scully.

"I suppose so," I said. I wanted to be by myself. "Thank you."

I couldn't sleep that night. The sun going down made no difference. For a long while, there wasn't enough air to breathe. The weird blood swarmed in my chest, and I longed for morning. Not only that, the story stuck to every part of me: to my body with its scales, my mind with its waves and silver flashes, and my soul with its homesickness.

Scully Slevin is a true seer, and a honey-tongue with it. He has a word hoard bigger than any wrecker's haul, and he sees things nobody else does. That needs no proof. You only have to see and hear him to know what he says is true.

Proof is for those with no eyes or ears in their heads.

CHAPTER FIVE

Gorge

MY NEW KNOWLEDGE BUBBLED in my chest, busting to be told, and my heart itched to be right. In the morning Ushag was nowhere to be found, though, and so I couldn't tell her. The barley meal hardened in the pot, the threshold was unswept, and Breck lowed pitifully down at the byre. As I shuffled through the yard, it was again already too hot. There was not a sigh of wind. At the byre, I let Bo in with her mother and watched awhile. Then I went and sat in the water barrel to think about the rest of the day.

In spite of her haggishness and the manner in which she daily left me wrung out with her small-mindedness, it was strange at home without my aunt. I needed to go somewhere else for the day; somewhere cool, plainly, and somewhere I might find food for our stores. We'd eaten most of the smoked fish and only had a little pig meat left. Ushag had mentioned going eel bagging up the gorge together soon, so I thought I'd do that. It was cooler up there, and later I could grab a bag of twilight eels and avoid her accusations of being a slugabout, while still spending the day in and around the river. My story would have to wait.

I grabbed the lumpen barley meal from the pot. It had set and was easy to eat while walking. I was just out of the yard when Bo skipped up beside me. She didn't understand when I pointed at the byre and told her to go back, so I had to lead her myself and shut the door on her. She watched with wet brown eyes as I walked away to the end of the path, and without a sound. We had always gone about together since she was only a few weeks old. Sometimes it was just to sit on the cliff edge and watch the sea, and sometimes to Market-Shipton, where she spent her time robbing apples or charging at the cattle sellers if they came too close. She was sweet and funny and everything—but doting on a cow suddenly seemed childish.

"Don't look at me like that!" I shouted at her, and I thought, *What is the matter with everybody?* "You're a cow!"

It was comforting to reach the shore, to hear the waves and feel the slippery sand and smooth pebbles under my feet. I did think for a moment that I should just go sit on the seabed, where it's always cool and peaceful, but I didn't want to be disturbed by all that coming up for air. I wished, as I often did, that I could breathe underwater. The sand gave way to pebbles under my feet. I stopped for a moment to shuffle about in their coolness.

I once saw some feet on folk in Shipton and almost brought up my meal at the sight. These folk commonly wore shoes but had taken them off to walk on the sand. It was like watching slugs, and made me look at my own quite differently. I like my feet. They're wide and brown and strong-looking.

Ushag had once made us shoes, but neither of us had been able to walk in them, so now they held sweet peas by the threshold in spring. We'd never laughed so much as watching each other try to walk in those shoes. Auntie Ushag couldn't bring herself to lift her feet at all. I lifted my whole leg, slow and careful-like, while gripping the shoe with my toes, but it still flew off. My aunt had laughed until she cried.

That had been a few years ago, but I still smiled to remember it. I thought it was comical too, but not so as you'd need to cry.

I scrambled up the stony riverbed where it snaked between the rock walls rising on each side of me. Wind is broken up and scattered by these walls, so it's always still up the gorge. Trees grow straight out from the cliff and then turn and stretch for the light, growing thin and long that way. Vines hang from the trees, and tiny green things grow where the river meets the stone. They look like mats of clover and even have flowers. Inside the flowers live little bright green ants.

As I climbed, the walls closed in. The rock holds the heat near the gorge entrance, but farther up, the sun cannot reach into the abyss, and I began to feel the warmth drain away. In the shadow of the cliff, I grew cool. I liked the feeling of my legs walking hard, my feet in the river, and my breath drawing in, cool, then flowing out, warm. My heart was pounding but my mind silent. In this manner I kept clambering upward.

At about noon I was higher than I had ever been, and it was all new country to me. The cliff walls were only four or five paces apart now, and the wide, slow river was a deeper stream splashing itself against boulders and flowing under ledges, down into the earth. Holes and gaps opened in the rock, and there were caves all around me.

The caves were marked by deep carvings all around their openings. I'd seen smooth hand-sized stones carved with just the same circles and spirals and shapes all over the headland. They just lie around and turn up wherever you dig, but I'd never seen the marks so deep and clear.

Some people say the smaller stones are the relics of the Old days, when the rock and cliffs were the business and property of those who lived inside the earth. Nobody knows who those folk were, but they are supposed to have liked digging, smithing, and carving. On the other hand, the Little Brothers say their god put the carvings in the rock at the very beginning of time for his own good reasons, and it's not for us to ask questions about his world but only to be grateful. Ushag says they're for the healing of women's problems and dizziness.

But these rocks were boulders. They couldn't be carried as pocket tokens or crushed to a powder and drunk. They were too big. One of the caves had a long tunnel as its opening and was marked by one deep-cut spiral.

Stooping to see but blinded by the sunlight, I doubled over to shuffle through the tunnel. As I did so, I left the light, and what I realized now had been warmth, behind me. It was cold like early winter inside the mountain. A strong smell of minerals, iron, and salt made me wrinkle my nose. When I stood up, I was in a small cave, dark but not pitch-black, and almost twice my height to its roof. I waited for the darkness to settle and then felt my way in. It wasn't far to the back wall, only a few steps with my arms stretched in front of me. I sat down with my back to the rock and my eyes to the tunnel entrance, from where a little light pierced and spread.

Damp stained the rock walls. My shoulders were already clammy. I could hear the river running underground, somewhere close but hidden. All was dark and dripping. Then something long and feathery crawled across my foot.

When I'm scared, I can't move. Other people jump or run, and that is the sensible way; I know it, but I can't do it. When I'm scared, I freeze. I hold my breath. I turn to stone. Anything could carry me off, or even kill me, while I stand there with mind and heart rushing but a body petrified.

So I froze. Only my eyes shifted. I'm ashamed, but it took all my courage just to look down at the long thing crawling across my feet.

It was only some long white worm with countless legs. Not deadly. I breathed again, and as I watched, it flattened itself and slid away into a crack in the cave wall. Lifting my eyes, I realized then that not just the white worm but the whole wall was moving. This cave was anything but empty. I half fell, half scrambled away from the living wall.

There were white spiders with legs ten times the length of their bodies, tiny pale hoppers with feelers as long as a hand, and there were all the slender, perfect toadstools. A frog whose eyes were as black and bulging as its body was wasted and sallow gulped at the clouds of grain-sized midges I'd disturbed, which now clouded my head and shoulders. There were water nymphs without wings. I waved and slapped at the biting midges, but they only rose in greater numbers. I sat still, and they settled again on thick slime-weed growing where damp wall met slippery floor.

Those white spiders hung from the wall on their impossible legs and blew about in any slight breath of moving air. I saw that the frogs were all blind, in spite of their bulging eyes, and so were the hoppers. It seemed a type of miracle that they should all be living there together inside the earth, and I sat and watched them a long time.

Slowly I got used to them; slowly I brought myself to look away. After a while I heard something bubbling in the far corner of the cave. I crawled over to it, feeling my way across the rough floor. I pulled myself up and over a rock rim and peered into a pool of black water. A face with searching black eyes peered up at me. I froze.

A savage face rose above a bony neck and shoulders and was tangled all about with a lot of dark hair. It stared at me. I stared at it. Neither of us shifted even a jot. Something slithered pale at the bottom of the black water, and I pulled back slightly. So did the face in the pool. I craned forward again. So did the face.

It was me.

I couldn't remember the last time I'd seen myself, but I hadn't looked like this. There was a stranger in my face, a look in the corner of my eye I didn't know. It was a hard face, with tight lips. I knew it from somewhere. *Ushag's face,* I thought, and sat back with my hand in the icy water and a few tears hot on my cheeks. The wind had picked up, and tiny gusts rolled about the cave, sending the spiders flying on their threads and disturbing the midges.

Then I heard them singing.

Just like Scully said, it wasn't a beautiful sound. It wasn't really what you'd call musical. It came from far away, and sounded like all the wild things at once: foxes, eagles, wasps, dolphins, barnacle geese, crickets. It also sounded like all the creatures caught and shut up in sheds and byres and fields and cages everywhere: lowing cattle, braying donkeys, howling dogs, and yowling cats. There was a chuckle of morning birds and the wailing of gulls in it too. It made me want to stand in the cave and make the same sound, to sing that song that was so free. It made me want to run. It made me want to fly from the cliff and land in the throat of the unseen singer.

It made me want my mother.

How can you want something you don't know? I thought, but the doubt didn't change the feeling. I still wanted her. I wondered, *Did she look like Ushag too?* Why had Ushag whispered and shaken her head when she said I was like my mother? How was I like her? Why was that a bad thing?

The singing stopped. Bubbles rose to the surface of the pool and popped. I'm not sure what I was expecting, but my heart wanted another face to be in there, a face like mine but older, a face with long, dangling earlobes and greenish skin. Instead, I just saw an eel. Not just any eel, either, but a huge, fat one that'd take plenty of smoking and plenty of eating. At once, my belly took charge of my heart, and I threw myself at it. It was a giant. I shouted as I fought to hold the coiling tail, and the water thrashed and foamed. It was such a battle as could shake the earth. I fell, and the eel slipped out of my hand.

The earth was shaking.

All the rubble and steeps were rocking. The earth-shakes were growing stronger as the summer passed. All the creatures of the rock walls had slipped away into the gaps and cracks, leaving only me and the eel. There was a grumbling deep within the earth, and all the hair on my arms stood up and the back of my neck prickled. The eel dived down into the pool and was gone. If I didn't get out, I would be buried alive, and I began to run, but the stone floor shifted and I fell. I reached out to catch myself, and as I did so, all was still and quiet again. I just lay there, eyes closed, with my hand flat against the wall.

When I opened my eyes, I saw some kind of chalky picture under my hand. In fact, all around the bottom of the cave wall, and around the pool itself, there were these pictures. At first I thought they were a kind of sea lily or anemone, but they weren't. They were outlines of hands. There seemed to be hundreds of them. The hand I'd reached out to when I was falling was smaller than the others. At first I thought it might be a child's hand. But when I looked closer at the fingers, I saw I was wrong. Those fingers changed everything.

Because they were webbed.

CHAPTER SIX

Kraken

I'D FOUND PROOF. My aunt would have to believe me, and then, in turn, she'd have to tell me what she was hiding from me, and then I would know it all. The true history of my mother was close; I could feel it. I ran home in twilight, forgetting the eel bag and slicing my feet open on old barnacles and broken shell all the way down the gorge. The blood trailed behind me across the sand, but I was numb to everything but this: I couldn't wait to tell it all right to her face! My scales. Merrow song. Webbed hands. She'd have to own I was right.

But Ushag didn't come home that night. I milked Breck and turned the cheese wheels, and ate my cold supper alone. Wherever she'd gone, my aunt had taken the last of the rushes, so I slept outside in the moonlight along with the night birds. I lay awake a long time, until the midnight wind-rise, and then slept, only to dream over and over of white webbed hands rising from a black pool. Ushag came home at daybreak.

Not seeing that I lay against the house rolled in a rug, she clattered into the yard, hung about with what looked like all our nets and snares, and dropped them in the dust by the well before taking a long draft from the bucket. She had more rabbit and fowl hanging about her middle than a deserted grain store. Their blood dripped and dribbled down her, front and back. She turned her face to the near-full moon, and I could see she'd been tying one on.

Every now and then, she does that. She sits by the fireplace, or goes alone to the grove of bees, and she drinks too much. Sometimes she drinks so much, she falls over and sleeps right where she is without moving a limb all night and wakes up with her face marked with the pattern of the ground. Sometimes she sings a little. I could see this night had been one of those nights.

She drank deeply from the well bucket and finally tipped the whole thing over her head. Then she hung the game in the lean-to and went to bed, and I went back to my webbed dreaming. I wanted her sober and well-rested to hear my proof, and to eat her humble pie.

But I slept until the sun was high, almost to noon, and when I woke, my aunt had gone again. She'd left me a bucket of wrens to pluck, having skinned and gutted the rabbits herself before she left. I did so and then saw to Breck and Bo, turned the cheese wheels, and put the meal in to soak. I swept the floor of the house, and watered the lean-to of its blood and feathers. When Ushag came home, she would have nothing to roll her eyes over, nothing to moan about at all, and then I would tell her.

By then it was midafternoon. I hoed the rows, spread the nets for the moon catch out in the sun, made a small-birds pie — and I was done in. I went to the rocks to sit and watch.

From these rocks overlooking the cove beach, with the gorge and the little inlet to my right and the red cliffs away to my left, I could see my whole world. I used to go there to look and be peaceful, but lately I went to wonder if there was ever to be any place for me other than this cove, its gorge, and the inlet. With no notion of where or what those other places might be, there was still something about this wide view of everything I knew that made me want more than I could see.

On cloudy days, the cliff stopped at the water-line. There was always something smashing or splintering against its base among the foam. Today there was some weird water moving along the cliff base. It seemed to be a river running its own private course within the sea itself. This sea-borne river was made of ruffled and bothered waters, and it passed under where I stood, rushing past me, the gorge, the little inlet, and out to sea. It coursed out beyond Carrick's waters, dragging foam, driftwood, and all kinds of wreckage. Far away, the undertow ended in a spiral of muck on the surface of the sea.

This tow was sucking everything into it. Near the inlet, the waters collected themselves somewhat, only to build and bubble there awhile and then burst out even stronger on the other side. There, in that protected beach, part of the rock wall had given way, and over the rubble I could see entirely into the cliff. Yesterday's earthshake had brought some of it down, and now there was a new sea cave. From where I stood, it looked to be deep.

I coveted that inlet and its new sea cave. It called me.

Down below me, the lone seal and her pup played in and out of the undertow. The mother was wise and swam across the tow, enjoying being swept away for a time and then collecting herself farther along. The pup followed her, as thoughtless as any land puppy and in danger of smashing his head any number of times, except that the mother wouldn't allow it. She nudged at him, steered him with her body, and when necessary, she rose right under him and carried him on her back into safe waters.

They barked and spat just like land dogs in a swift stream. I wanted to live in the salty water just like them, and to twist and roll through the waves like they did. I wanted to rise and fly, spitting at the sun. I wanted to be part of the wild play, but I was too scared of being carried away into the sea in a sort of Progress, along with the rest of the tow's wreckage.

Then I saw Ushag. She was standing in the twilight sea, fully dressed and unmoving. She was waist-deep right in my spot, right where I go to sit. *She's never where you want her to be,* I thought, *and always where you don't. Typical!* I could see even from the cliff that she was in one of her cold, dry humors.

So I couldn't go to tend my anemone gardens if I wanted, or to watch the herds of urchins graze in the sea meadows. I would have to pass my aunt, and I could see from her face, it wouldn't do. I didn't want to speak to her until she had the ears to hear me. I didn't want to see her until she stopped rolling her eyes. Suddenly I didn't care whether she came home that night or not. I set out for the Slevins'.

I didn't arrive until well after dark, and there was a bit of a fuss from Ma, who insisted on putting the pot back on the fire and sending Scully to relieve "poor Ushag's" worry. I assured them that my aunt was a cold fish who thought of nothing but work, and they didn't need to waste one thought for her, but Ma crossed herself and fussed about her altar, and was generally so hurt that I said sorry and hugged her before there were tears.

"Your aunt has good reason for how she is." She sighed and passed me the broth and gobbets. I tasted it and straightaway knew how hungry I was.

"Well, I wish she'd tell me," I drawled through my full mouth, dripping broth and cabbage and fish. "She's so tight-lipped. I can't find out anything!" On the last word, I spat up a lump of fish and bone, sending Ma reeling back.

"Heishan!" Ma dabbed at her face and mine. "She'll tell you in her own good time. She's the fully grown woman in your house."

In an instant, I was at once flayed-red and white-hot. "Well, what am I, then?" Tears burst from the corners of my eyes. The fire hissed as some fell in the flames. "What am I, eh? I'm no child any longer, and nobody can say I'm not. I'm almost thirteen years old, and I do everything she does. And I do it by myself these days." Ma watched my face as I spoke. "I mean, she plainly knows I can do it all without her. What else is there to being grown?"

Ma squatted by her altar in her corner. She lit the tapers and placed the bits of spat-out fish in a hollow in some driftwood, and mumbled a blessing over it. I didn't know what she was doing, but Ma has her own ways, and if you leave her to them, you end up feeling soothed somehow. She poured fresh milk into two bowls and gave one to me. The other she offered to the set of fine cow horns that hang above everything else in Ma's corner.

"Poor Ushag," she said to the horns, sighing.

"What?" I spluttered.

"Mind the water!" she bawled, and threw the steeped remains of a brew out the door. "Ushag wasn't always so sour," Ma carried on. "She has a big heart—I know, I know. You can't see it. And have I not said to you that people only see that which they have the eyes to see and only hear what they have ears to hear? She has a big heart, and good hands like her father, who was a great one for the work. It was him who made the Marrey place a real home. He built the outbuildings and laid out the plots nice and even and so on. Before him it'd been a wild sort of place and the family a half-wild lot. She was always more practical than her sister, and quicker to anger and argue, but I don't remember her being cold." Ma's eyes glazed over as the Ven and Ushag of twenty years before rose in her mind.

"If you don't mind me saying, Ushag's trouble is that she doesn't believe in anything anymore. That's no way for a body to live. After the thing with Ven, she did take to Jesus a little, but it didn't help, and then it didn't take long for her to fall out with the Little

Brothers over the failure, as she saw it. She kept way-laying them outside church and giving them three chances to tell her why Jesus hadn't heard her prayers for Ven and made it right."

"I can just see that," I said. The picture in my mind of my aunt, arms crossed and lips clamped, giving the monks three chances to prove their god's power tickled me.

"Eventually, they banned her from church ground." Ma looked impressed. "Monastery, chapel, and all. But she's only got her own soul and mind and heart to live with in this world—and her mind and heart are dark since . . . since the thing with the sister. I don't mean dark like evil, you know, or a home for the Old enemy. I only mean dark like empty, dark like unknown—"

"Like a cave," I suggested.

"That'll do," she said.

After the broth and the altar business, I felt altogether more peaceful. I settled in by the hearth and told Ma about the unnatural tow happening in our cove. "Ah, now," she breathed excitedly. "I could tell you something about that." She came closer to the flames and rocked on her heels. Her eyes sparkled.

I'd never known anybody for a story like Ma. She was even worse than me, in spite of her great age.

"Go on, then," I said.

"My brother, Bearnard," started Ma with her eyes

closed, "was a great one for fishing, even as a boy, and when he reached twelve, he was taken on by the best crew out of Shipton. He was older than me by ten years, so I didn't see him much, and during the Hungers he took to fishing the open ocean and was gone months at a time. He saw things out there and learned to read the water for its rising fogs and other sudden humors, and from a boy who could talk the devil down, he grew into a heavy, quiet man we saw only every few years. But he told me all about the tow in Marrey Cove."

I didn't think I'd ever get used to hearing Ma and Scully call our place Marrey Cove.

"There was a great swell on the north headland in those days, such as hadn't been seen in memory. The waves beat right up the cliff, and each one took a slab back to the sea with it. Monstrous tides filled the caves and crashed halfway up the gorge. At high tide, a longshore undertow ripped at the cliffs and beach and stormed out to sea. Most folk stayed away, as you might think was wise, but Bearnard was captain of his own vessel now, and he took the *Margaid* and her crew around there, and all on purpose. Curiosity was always the main part of him.

"On the day he went north, a whirlpool opened in the mouth of the cove. Anchored just without, the crew could still feel the drag in the spinning waters. At first the men laughed and felt a pleasure in the sea's power, but when the anchor began to break free from its holdfast and the boat to tremble and move toward the whirlpool, it was a different story altogether. Now the men were silent, and greasy with fear.

"It was one of those times when human skill and desire add up to nothing, and the sea shows its true face; neither mother nor lover is it, but only heartless water and wind. The *Margaid* picked up speed, and the closer the ship was sucked to the edge of the whirlpool, the louder the ship's boards strained. The crew seemed all for drowning, and my brother always said that was the moment he made peace with his gods. In fact, he came forward to the bow and was prepared to ride it out as the line ran to its bitter end. So the creaking hull was drawn into the cove and into the spinning waters.

"That ship crept right up to the edge of the whirlpool, where constantly the waves fell over its terrible rim. Now Bearnard and the rest could look right over the edge and into its depth, and he did so, though he never thought he'd bring back what he saw to land and folk.

"But with the luck of the brave and good on him, the anchor was, even in this last moment, gripped on the seabed by something fixed and strong enough to hold—and the creaking ship stopped and held its position. Hanging on the edge by their one thin line, all praying and some crying out for their mothers by now, every man jack of them looked straight down into a whorl of water that opened to the very seafloor itself."

With Ma's singsong chanting and the fire dying, I lay back in the straw and sacking and closed my eyes. I could see in my mind's eye the hole in the sea to its very floor, and the tiny ship perched on its edge.

"Are you sleeping?" Ma asked me accusingly. She poked at the flames, and then threw the stick on the fire. "Or perhaps it's not your kind of story?"

I opened my eyes. "I'm listening," I said.

"Good, because my brother told me in his own words what he saw, and I won't be wasting them on ears belonging to them who don't want to know. I learnt Bearnard's words off by heart so I could say it just as he would. He said, 'A monstrous beast was descending to the base of the unsoundable whirlpool, watching us with one huge bulging eye. He had so many long, flailing legs, I could count no more of them after eighteen, and each one was studded with hooks and spikes and tentacles. Two beaks he clicked at us, the horrible double-mouthed monster, one on each side of his head, and as I studied further, I saw four eyes. As many fish circled him in the whirling water as stars circle the night sky, and he fed from them as he felt, and still they circled. He was the kraken, and a king in his own land. The fish gave themselves to him.' These were Bearnard's very words.

"Well, as is the way with these accounts, the second mate later recalled a head like a cat, and the sixth mate insisted that all the legs they'd seen had really been a constantly writhing body—the kraken being more like a python than anything else, and that its head was more cow-like than cattish. The one thing they all recalled likewise, though, and it's not surprising, as they were fishermen, was the beast's attendant court of fish.

"As the kraken settled into his lair, the whirlpool began to close. Starting at the seafloor, the waters rushed and fell together once more. The poor *Margaid* rocked and leaped upon its rim, and as the last waves collided and sent a fountain up, water, weed, fish, and the ship all danced in the air together before falling back to the sea with a slap. The great court of fish stayed in the Marrey Cove for a week after, and Bearnard and the others all filled their nets. It was the best catch in history."

I was tired now and wondered how many more stories I hadn't heard. The weight of what I didn't know was heavy upon me. "Are you telling me there's a kraken living in our cove?" It seemed to me to be the sort of thing my aunt should have told me.

"I'm telling you to go fishing tomorrow," said Ma.

CHAPTER SEVEN

Moonfish

I DIDN'T GET HOME UNTIL TWILIGHT the following day. Ushag met me on the path. She was hung all about with nets and pails, and carried the grappling hook we'd found washed up last spring. My aunt couldn't meet my eyes, and I found myself flushing and shuffling too, though I'd done nothing wrong. I noticed she was pale, with great dark rings around her eyes, and her hands shook as she gripped the tackle. *That's what you get for climbing into the mead jar for two days,* I thought. Maybe she takes after Doolish and the others whose answer to every question is a brew.

I gave her the scornful eye.

Ushag pointed at the cove with the hook. "They're in," was all she said, and as I looked into the cove, I could see she was right. The shallows flashed silver with fish. She started down the cliff, and then paused and met my eyes for a moment. Moon fishing had always been pleasurable work to us. Each month of the summer, we'd watch the moon wax and wait on the night when we could stand in the dark water, knee-deep in mackerel and their light wakes. My aunt raised an eyebrow at me, and her eyes reminded me of Bo's when I sent her back to the byre. I saw the dark shadows under them, and the scar by her mouth from that time she'd chewed the hide for our shoes. All winter she'd chewed until they were soft enough, and then all we'd done was fall over in them and laugh.

Against my will, I was sorry for her.

But she's the one who's wrong! I thought. *She's the hold-back, the cold one. The liar.*

In spite of being right, though, I nodded, and with that, we had a sort of truce. We did need the fish.

The night was warm, as they had been for so long now that it felt like we'd never be cold again, and so still it was as if it were holding its breath. The sea shone silver and rolled heavily, the waves bulging but never breaking. Only ripples hissed up the sand and back, as though the cove had never known such a thing as a storm. There was the stench of weed and suchlike rotting in the heat.

Each taking one end of the gill net, we waded into the silky water. These days it was warmer to swim at night than during the day. Everything was back-to-front. The sea mirrored the moon and stars, and showed us our own faces staring back at us, but there was no seeing below its surface. We could only feel the mackerel as they slipped around our ankles. Even standing right in it, it kept its secrets from us. We stood and rocked at the knees awhile, and then Ushag rolled up her sleeves and nodded to me.

I rolled the net into her hands and stood back as she hurled. It seemed to unpack itself into the air. My aunt always had a powerful throwing arm. In the likeness of a wing, it flew straight and perfect until it fell flat on the surface, where it held itself for a moment. Then it sank, leaving only the floaters and the line.

She was truly a great hurler. Against my will, I couldn't help admiring it. *A good chuck doesn't mean a good character,* I thought. *She keeps secrets that are none of hers to keep.*

She gave me the line, and I tied it to my wrist. Taking the hand net then, she walked a little away and stood unmoving, watching the starlight and moonwake on the water. Every now and then, she'd swoop the net and bring it up wriggling. Our pails began to fill. I waited for the gill net to settle. It had floated on the longshore tow around the rocks and into the still water beyond. I couldn't see many of the floaters any longer, but all I had to do was wait for the line to twitch and struggle and then haul in a feast.

I waited.

My aunt was small and silent in the bright moonlight, and her hair hung straight and black to her middle. She stood so long with her face to the sea, I had the fancy she was a carving, and a bad-tempered one at that, with her sharp nose and jaws either clenching or chewing on nothing.

I watched her face for a long time, and then I asked, "How am I like her?"

Straightaway her body sagged. "Neen, stop it," she said. Anybody would think I didn't have a right to know about my own mother.

I watched her as she swept another flashing net into the bucket. "Was she like you?"

"No."

This answer was like some small victory, and I was emboldened. "How was she different?" I pushed my little bit of luck.

Ushag looked out to the horizon. I could see her thinking.

"She was never content. She was full of fancies." She sighed. "Her head was filled with stories . . . and she never learned to work properly."

She heaved her full bucket onto the nearby rocks and had to come close by me to do so. "Is that why you didn't like her?" I asked.

Ushag didn't answer me but only pressed her lips together and studied the ripples as they slipped up the beach. "I never said I didn't like her," she said. My mouth dried out, and suddenly I was too hot.

"Well, why did you even bother, then?" I heard my voice start to shrill again.

"Bother to what?" my aunt asked, and I could see she was in the dark.

"Why did you bother staying?"

Ushag looked me straight in the eye. "Do you see another aunt around here?" She pulled at the net a little, hand over hand over hand. "It's all very well for her . . ." she muttered at the sea. "She and the merrows, and all that lot, have it all over me. I have to make do with being a regular person."

Honor Bright, even when she answers, who can tell what she means? I would have pushed her for more, but the gill net started to tug and nearly yanked me off my feet. Ushag dropped her hand net and waded to my side. We hauled side by side, and gradually the net came back around the rocks and into sight. It was heavy, plainly full of a good catch. Straightaway my heart rose, and I couldn't help whooping a bit.

"Ma said to go fishing tonight," I told Ushag as we hauled. "I told her about the undertow, and she said it was the kraken calling his court together, and that we should go get our nets. She told me the whole thing." My aunt's face, as she leaned back against the weight of the net and listened to me, was shining with sweat, but its expression didn't change a jot. "And we did—and look!" I added, leaning backward to help drag it all in. "We must have caught his whole court . . ." As the net came in, we saw not only fish but red crabs, conches, feathers, claws, and pinchers. "And some hangers-on!" I laughed, picking out a sunfish and holding it up to the moon.

"Oh, for crying out loud!" shouted Ushag.

Without warning, I was laughing a little, and then laughing a lot. My aunt took no notice, for which I was grateful, because I couldn't stop. I tried holding it in, but it bust out with a spit and a howl and the tears rolling down my cheeks. The howls at last turned to sobs, but then the hiccoughs started. For a time I was laughing and crying at the same time, like some mad person. I felt my face crumple like a child's, and now I couldn't stop crying. My aunt glared at the sea. We kept hauling at the net.

Fist over fist we dragged in and bucketed mackerel and wrasse, crab and eel, and hand over hand we threw back weed and moon jellies, urchins and sea squirt. We don't like eating urchins; too salty, too slimy, and too much work for not enough reward. I worked hard and felt myself drain of the full-moon humor that had me behaving like a body could hold both tears and laughter at the same time. Picking over the net bit by bit and sorting what was there, my aunt finally spoke.

"The kraken," she told me, "is a story the family told outsiders to keep them away from the cove. In the old days."

My aunt had some type of Unbelieving sickness. It was like she was determined not to believe me, or anybody, or anything, and no matter what. Ushag was older than me, and that meant I should believe her, but Ma Slevin was older than her, and so Ushag should believe Ma. I was about to put her straight about this deformity of hers and tell her all about the cave of hands and the merrow song when, somewhere out of sight, the last length of gill net became snagged. We tugged at it, but it wouldn't budge, so Ushag swam around the rocks to disentangle it.

A few moments later, there was a sharp cry like a gull's. I pulled again at the net, and it came free with a jerk. The next set of ripples in the widening moon-wake showed Ushag inside the net itself, holding on to something I couldn't see but that was plainly precious. I pulled her and it into the shallows and ran to see what she had.

We'd caught a plague of jellies and their stingers. These red and tangled stingers can float for a furlong behind the creature, and even ripped away from their bodies, they leave a body welted and feverish. Ushag was using a stick to get rid of them from all about her, flicking them back into the sea. Then she was just sitting there, all skirted with weed, floaters, and net, and she was holding, in her arms, a man.

If he was a man, that is. He was long, almost impossibly long, and his hair was yellow and sticking to a blue body all the way to his waist. From the whiteness of his lips and this blue body, I thought that if he was a man, he was a Dead one, but then he moaned. Ushag slapped him softly on his cheeks and chest and asked him to speak, but he didn't. He just rolled his eyes up into his head until all we saw were the whites. Then I saw he wasn't blue; he was covered head to toe in skin pictures. There were fish swarming across his shoulders, waves breaking up his arms, ships sailing his chest and on his belly, an anchor and line, a wolf's head by his hip, and, farther down, secret marks of some kind.

He was bare, entirely.

He was too tall for Ushag to manage alone, so together we heaved him up the shoreline onto the sand and untangled him from the net and its wreckage. I ran up to the house and brought back a cover for him, and the jug. We poured a little mead into him and sat him up with the cover about his shoulders. By the bright moonlight, we could see he'd been terribly stung, and had received a buffet to the head that had broken the skull somewhat. I felt sick at it, but also he'd been nibbled about the toes and fingers by the fish.

With all the mead in him, we half dragged, half carried him up to our place, and most of the carrying part I did. I'm taller than Ushag now, and he fit my shoulder better. It was strange to have this naked man leaning against me all the way up to the yard. I didn't know where to look, but what could I do? I was proud to be able to hold his weight, and it would have been worse somehow for him to have to lean on Ushag.

We put him in the cow byre with Breck and Bo. I made a bed of clean straw, and we laid him in it. Ushag brought out the new rabbit-and-hare rug and covered him. She brought out her box of cures and simples. Then we lit the rushes and looked him over closely.

He was a terrible sight. His lips were white and split, and his eyes swollen top and bottom so that they were only slits in his face. He looked like he'd been dragged over a barnacle bed with his limbs all sliced and bruised; there wasn't an unscraped spot left on him, but his poor body had given up on bleeding and the ragged edges of his wounds had grown grey. His toes and fingers had puffed up like sea squirts. As he dried, his body grew more rimed with salt. My aunt rubbed her hands together, opened her box, and started bustling about.

The palest of blue eyes stared out from within the near-drowned man's swollen face and watched. Once, his lips opened and let out a small dry sound. I bent down to hear him, and he grasped my arm and mumbled something in a rasping, lumpy talk. I put my ear to his mouth.

"*Ískaldr,*" he breathed, and fell back, still gripping my arm. As I loosed his fist from my arm, I saw the figure of a merrow on it. Its tail circled his wrist, and its flowing hair held ships and whales and smoking pipes.

I went back to the beach to fetch the catch. It took me until well past midnight, and when I came home, Ushag had bathed the blue man's wounds. She was sitting by him as he suffered from a Recurring Senselessness. She sat by him all night, combing the grit and tiny crabs out of his long yellow hair.

CHAPTER EIGHT

Water Horse

AUNTIE USHAG FILLED THE BLUE MAN with cowslip and masterwort, and after he'd puked and was dead to the world, she bathed him in wolfsbane and yarrow. Calmly, she bound his eyes with blessed thistle and sprinkled powdered bloodstone into his head wound, and then said that to really help him she needed her old bone stones, but she'd lost those years ago. She said she thought he'd broken his nose and, as if she did it every day, she stuffed a mustard ball up each nostril, saying that would have to do for now. They made a sickening grating sound as they went in.

She filled the room with her busyness. Breck and Bo chewed their cud and watched her curiously. I listened to the insensible man trying to suck air through his broken nose, and suddenly I'd had enough of sick rooms, silence, and cow shit.

"Ma has a pile of healing stones around the—"
I nearly said "altar" but changed my mind at the last
moment. "Hearth," I finished. I didn't know any
longer how my aunt would feel about anything. "I'll
go fetch them, shall I? There's all sorts."

Ushag nodded without looking up from the man,
and I went.

It was dawn-break as I left the yard, and it took me
until midmorning to get to the Slevins' place. Scully
was grinding their meal by the well, talking to himself under his breath. As I came close, he just raised
his voice and talked to me instead. "I was just saying
we have a visitor from the monastery," he said. "The
Prior himself has come to save my mother from herself. Listen . . ."

The Prior of the Little Brothers of Perpetual
Patience was preaching in a rumbling voice to Ma
about her altar. I could tell he'd had time to sink to his
most deep and impressive tones. Ma's own voice was
high-toned and getting higher. Right now she sounded
somewhat like an albatross.

"I can't be taking away old Breeshey's bowl, Father,
and you shouldn't ask it."

"Our Lord doesn't want you worshipping other
gods, Mary dear, and you know it. He's jealous of
other gods."

"Breeshey's not a god! She's a . . . well . . . she's

just Breeshey. And she's been living here in those horns since before you came, and I can't just ask her to go now. It'd be terrible unthankful." Ma paused and added sulkily, "Jesus has never asked it of me in any of our little talks, and if he can see my point, I don't see why you can't."

"The Lord Jesus wants you down at the chapel, and living the good and Christian life so you can be with him in heaven. Don't you want to go to heaven, Mary?"

Ma looked at him suspiciously. "Well, now . . . that depends on who's going to be there?" she asked. "I mean, apart from the lovely boy Jesus, that is."

"All the good, Christian souls you've ever known will be there," said the Prior brightly.

Ma's face didn't change a jot, but her eyes glazed over.

"All those poor babies of yours," he added with a cheerful smile, but she just looked sadly out the door. I knew she was thinking of the Other things they'd buried in her children's graves. She saw me standing in the shadows listening and pulled me inside with relief.

"Here's Neen Marrey from the cove, Father. Her aunt is that Ushag Marrey who gave you the troubles a few years back. Say hello to the Father, Neen." She gripped my hand and didn't let go.

"Hullo, Father," I said.

The Prior didn't exactly give me the glad eye.

"Hello, Neen Marrey."

I grew restless under his gaze. In spite of his crusted habit and a tongue and beard red from wine, he made me feel dirty. He looked at me like I was planning something lawless and indecent, and if he could look long and hard enough he'd find what it was in my face. He found nothing, though, and turned back to Ma.

"The Return is expected any day now, Mary—we're all getting ready down at the Abbey—and I do want to see you and your unlucky boy in Glory. I believe I'd miss you too much if you weren't there." His eyes twinkled at her. She twinkled back as though she couldn't help it. "You know you're my favorite pagan. Ha! Ha!" His laugh gave Ma a chance to drag the talk back into our world.

"You're a terrible man, and I shouldn't be surprised if they don't stop you at the gate of your very own heaven with all your . . . ways." She smiled broadly through the black stubs of her teeth.

At once, they both turned to me expectantly. I'd been struck somewhat disgusted by the aged flirting, and I had to be elbowed by Ma to find my tongue. "What?" she asked me.

"Ushag says to say we've fished a man up in the gill net and he's broken his nose and can we have any bone stones you have lying about?" I asked in a rush.

"A man is hurt!" shrilled Ma, and the Prior jumped. "Why didn't you speak up straightaway?" She started cramming the stones into a bag. "I'll come with you. Father, you'll have to excuse us." She stood up. "A man is hurt. We're off." She was hopping about like a robin in her relief.

The Prior stepped forward and took the rattling bag off Ma's shoulder. "I'll be coming too," he said, and patted her hand. "Maybe I can help in some small way."

Ma swapped the irritated eye with me, but there was no refusing him. Scully joined us, and even with us making slower time because of Ma and the old Prior, we were back at our yard by midafternoon. There's nothing like pure curiosity to drive the oldest, the sickest, and the slowest legs.

When I'd set out, the day had again looked to be settling in hot and skyclad, and it was with thankfulness that on our way to the roundhouse, the sky mottled and an onshore breeze picked up. There was even some dark cloud out at the horizon. Maybe it would rain tonight and all the overhot humors of the last weeks would cool. We arrived just as the lightning and thunder started up.

Auntie Ushag came into the yard to look at the sky. Her eyes narrowed at the sight of the Prior, but she nodded civilly enough at him. I had secretly hoped for sharp words at least, and possibly even fists, but he just nodded civilly back. It was a shame. I'd have put my money on Auntie Ushag getting the better of him any day.

"Now, now. Here we are, here we are." Ma headed off my aunt and, taking the rattling bag off the Prior, led the way into the byre. One by one, we four squeezed ourselves into the tiny sage-sharp room, pushing the protesting cows out of the way. In the blaze of almost all our store of tapers and rushes, Ma leaned over the sleeping man. She studied his face and lifted the rug from his torso.

Standing up slowly, she turned and folded her hands over her belly.

"He's a wiggynagh," she said. I didn't know what she meant. "A man from up in the north," she explained. She swapped a quick look with Ushag. "And a fine-grown one at that."

Ushag's face stayed cold. "Maybe under all the muck," she said, tipping up the bag of bone stones and laying them out.

When all the stones were on the ground, we found a few that looked like noses. There were some like fingers, some like hips, and others like knees or elbows. There were a pile of broken bronze shells. One even looked like a giant stone beetle, but I don't know what you'd use that for. Ma and Ushag chose the likeliest nose stone and carefully tied it to the man's face. At this, he began to stir, and the two women watched as he slowly regained his senses.

"He looks like a raider," said the Prior, pushing forward. "He has the height, the scars. And the look of killing about him. Where did he come from?"

"From my gill net," said Ushag shortly.

"Why's he so white and yellow?" I asked.

Under his skin pictures, he was as white as the Prior's collar, and his hair was yellow like primroses. Nobody on Carrick looked like that; we were all darkhaired, or red. Though plainly the others had heard of his people, I'd never been told about them.

"His folk live with the ice and snow. They have no sunlight in winter, and nothing but sunlight in summer," said the Prior, as if he were saying a lesson. "They grow so tall to be nearer the sun in summer. Their pale skin sucks in all that season's light and heat, and stores it in their hair. That light and heat is then released through the dark winters, allowing the pale races to survive that crisis."

We all looked around at the others. Nobody seemed convinced. I looked to Ushag, but she just shrugged and raised her eyes to heaven.

"He's awake," said Scully just then.

I turned, and the Northman's startling and skyclad eyes were looking straight at me. Those eyes were like slits of blue sky, and not common blue sky either, but the kind of skies we'd had recently, so pale as to be almost white. He opened his cracked, balm-daubed lips, and I thought he smiled at me.

"*Njótið heilir handa,*" he croaked, and reached out one huge hand toward me. He tried to say something more but choked instead. So he put his hand on his heart and smiled at me. His split lips bled a little. "*Góð píka . . .*"

"Look out." The Prior hopped forward into the light and stood between me and the Northman. "He's saying 'girl.' They're blood-soaked, war-wise men, this lot. They have no respect for women."

"You seem to know a lot about him and his people, for a priest who came to us beardless and hasn't left Carrick since," Ushag snapped, lifting a cup of burdock and honey to the sick man's lips.

"We had a northern novice in my first posting," answered the Prior with no temper on show at all. "I was very young. I'm afraid I often found him more interesting than my prayers." There was a silence, in which the Northman sipped and swallowed and made hoarse sounds in his throat. "He told such stories! I learned a little of their language and ways."

"*Hefir þú sét skip?*" the Northman said, lifting himself on one elbow.

"He's asking about his raid ship," translated the Prior.

"We saw no ship," Ushag replied, and squatted by his bed. She shook her head vigorously. "No ship. Only you." She pointed her finger at his chest. The Northman seemed to understand. He lay back in the rabbit-and-hare rug and sighed. I thought it a sigh of relief.

"These men worship only war," the Prior went on importantly. "The northern novice couldn't stand to be without his weapons and war weeds. In the end, he killed the cook and left us in the middle of the night." Under its scrapes and slashes, the Northman's face seemed kind to me. The Prior's face, on the other hand, had grown proud and a little cruel. "According to the bishop, the wiggynagh are to be swallowed up entirely in the last days . . . along with all witches and charmers and healers . . ." Ma, Scully, and I looked at the floor, but Ushag met his eyes, and he dwindled under her disgust. "And all the others . . ." he said, his voice dying away.

"Well, well, that's a lot of folk, Father," muttered Ma, giving Ushag the wary eye. "Just look at that sky. It's getting late now. You'd best be heading down, or you'll miss evening service."

The Prior had been pricked by Ushag's scornful eye and had found his preaching voice again. "Late, is it?" he began. "It's more than late, Mary. It's almost too late! The millennium is upon us, with all its incests and adulteries, its lies and frauds and self-loving ways."

"Honest, now, Father, none of us here love ourselves, so you just save your worry for those who need it." Ma tried to calm him, but he wasn't done yet.

"Did you hear, Mary, about the twins down at Strangers' Croft?"

Ma nodded. "Poor little mites," she said.

"Poor little mites, my elbow!" He leaned in toward her. "They're signs! Unnatural little twinned signs!"

I was all at sea. What was he talking about? And why was he calling Ma Mary? Her name is Mureal. He was like a madman. Ushag was furiously rolling torn cloths for bandage and pressing her lips together.

"We asked for signs, and now they're here. It starts. Those twins are only the beginning. There's reports through England of headless infants who eat their meal through their navels, and depraved, doubly sexed individuals getting themselves offspring alone. The signs are here all about us; some have skeletons outside their flesh or are furred all over, or fledged. There are even some who are gilled and webbed." His voice trembled with disgust. "There are those with scales dwelling among us." I hid my hands, and Ushag saw. She put her arm around my shoulder, and she was shaking and making fists.

"Go fetch a jug," she whispered to me.

"No," I said.

"The signs are all around us, but we won't read them," the Prior finished sadly.

"Well, that's quite a story, and I'll be sure to learn more of it another time," said Ma, fussing at his collar and cloak. "I'm thankful for your care of us, Father, I really am, but it's time for you to be at chapel. You'll be late and the congregation all let down if you don't leave right this moment." She took him firmly by the shoulder. "Thank you for all your help, and Scully will walk you safe to the path." She steered him toward the door. "You've been such a help to us poor women, and I'll surely be seeing you in the church . . ." He plainly didn't want to go. "Soon."

"I don't need your boy to see me safe. You know, maybe I should stay. That one there could be just biding his chance to loot you and . . ." He looked at me, then at my aunt. "And worse," he said meaningfully. Anybody would think I hadn't grown up with the wild animals and with the spring about me, with Breck and her seasonal bull, or that on drunken market days in town I went about blind. I knew what he meant.

"We can look after ourselves, man." Auntie Ushag tried to keep her voice low and calm but didn't quite manage it. Ma crowded the Prior toward the door, but it was too late. My aunt had lost her battle with her temper. "You can take your jealous god, and his milksop son . . ." she started, with Ma making little distressed noises and trying to cover his ears. She flapped her shawl like a crow at the Prior's head until she forced him out into the yard with Scully following and sniggering. A scarlet-faced Auntie Ushag followed them out into the yard, hands on hips and booming. "And your book of secret rules, and your thieving taxes, and child pope, and your dooms and signs, and you can shove them all right up your—" She stopped and took a long breath. "Your holy fundament," she said at last, and went back inside the byre.

Scully bust right out laughing. I slapped him on the back of the head. "Shhh!" I hissed, delighted. "What's a fundament?"

The Prior left, alone, and we all followed Ushag inside.

"I'm sorry," said Ushag, who was now white and trembling.

We all muttered that it was "all right," and "entirely understandable." And then Ma said, "What a day! We could all do with a meal and a brew."

She left Scully and Ushag and me sitting around the Northman as he slept, and when she came back with the mead jug and broth, I was almost asleep. We ate in silence, and drank drafts of the warm, sweet mead, and gently we all settled. The thunder had stopped, but it hadn't rained. There had been a red sky at sunset, so tomorrow would be clear and hot. We sat in a shrinking circle of light at the bed of the Northman, and it was as if we were the only beings in the world. Outside the light, anything could be happening, but inside the circle, we were as we ever were.

"You know, I heard a story once about a girl who fished a man out of a lake." Ma slipped a sly glance in my aunt's direction. My aunt sighed and rolled her eyes. "Oh, go on, Birdie," said Ma. "It's a good one."

There was no answer from Ushag, so Ma carried on. I felt myself drifting sleepily, like weed on the surface of water. There were clouds inside my head, then I was the clouds, and then I was the blue sky and the clouds just kept passing. The story came from far away.

"A girl was grazing her cattle at the High Lake when she came upon a man, soaked and bubbling from the mouth, by the water's edge. He was covered in weed, as yours is, Ushag Marrey, and he was big and brawny and so beautiful she decided she'd keep him, and she took him home on the back of one of her red cows. She nursed him back to life and then set the arrangements for a wedding.

"She'd only known him a month.

"The day before the wedding, she was up by the lake again, gathering wildflowers for her dress, when she came upon a frisky horse. A stallion it was, and big and beautiful, and she thought how marvelous her man would look sat up on this fine beast, and set about catching it for him.

"She tried offering it sweet grass. She tried skipping and circling in play all around it to awaken its curiosity. She tried ordering it to her side with the voice of command, and singing it to her side with the voice of the lark, but nothing worked. She sat on the edge of the lake and began to weep in frustration. That's when the horse, fickle and unpredictable creatures that they are, waded up to her in the shallows of the icy lake and nosed at her, and let her catch him.

"As soon as she had her hands in his thick mane, she leaped like a hare and swung her leg over him. She sat astride the beautiful horse and pointed his head toward home, no doubt dreaming of gratitude and reward. But the horse turned his mighty head to the lake, and nothing would turn him.

"With those powerful limbs beating and his mane turning to foam, he carried the girl into the deep black water of the lake. She tried slipping off, but her legs were now as one with the water horse, for that's what it was. She tried pulling its mane and beating its eyes to make it stop, but her hands only passed through its hair and flesh as through water. She tried begging to be freed, but the creature just turned and smiled, and that's when she recognized her own man, the man she'd taken home and fed and nursed only one month before.

"And in this terrible moment, the water horse carried the girl down into the High Lake. And, instead of him becoming her husband, she became the water horse's wife. And she was never seen again about the home place or the markets, and that was it and all about it."

Could this story be real? I thought it sounded as likely as any other story I'd heard: like the story of the kraken and the undertow, or the story of how Scully got his Othersight, or the story of Doolish Marrey and his merrow wife. This story, though, was different, and Ma seemed to be trying to tell Ushag something with it, but my aunt had stopped listening.

She was quietly heating her pot and tending the Northman as he slept.

CHAPTER NINE

Ulf's Story

ULF," SAID THE NORTHMAN, and hit his chest with his open hand.

My aunt and I gazed at him and then at each other with blank faces.

"Ulf! Ulf!" he repeated.

"Maybe he's sore," I said, and Auntie Ushag fetched more hawthorn. She tried to get him to take it, but he shook his head and grabbed her hand.

"Mik — uh . . . ul . . . fuh," he repeated, firmly laying her hand upon his head and hitting his own crown with it at each sound.

I tried passing him the pot. He'd suffered with a terrible double Flux all night, and I thought he might be hungry after such an emptying and scouring. He shook his head, though, and covered his face while sighing deeply. Sitting up as well as he could, he patted the bed next to him. I went to him and sat. He seemed to be setting himself to patience.

Giving me the meaningful eye and smiling gently, he touched his chest. Then he said very clearly, *"Ek heiti Ulfr."* I didn't understand him again and was sorry for it; his face was so hopeful and I, so curious for his story.

"I suppose so," I said as kindly as I could, and patted his shoulder.

That was the first day, when our Northman was such a stranger to us, and he seemed to be of another race than the race of men. It's silly now, but we weren't sure even what to feed him and were relieved when he tucked into his rabbit and skirrets. He was plainly a human, in spite of him being so long and yellow, but until we could share talk, I thought us doomed to be always strangers.

But he had given up on words and now he tried mimicry. Making the shape of waves breaking with his hands, he pointed out the door. "I suppose," I said, "it's the sea."

His eyes followed my lips. "Ahspose. Dahzee," he copied me. He curved his hand into the form of a cup and placed it upside down on his hand waves.

"A ship?" I said. "A ship on the sea." He laughed his first booming laugh, and it was catching. I laughed too.

"Uh shepun dahzee," he repeated. "Uh shep."

"Ship." I drew my lips back to make the middle sound. He watched my mouth.

"Sheeep," he said, and looked to me. He looked so content, I couldn't correct him again.

"That'll do," I told him.

He raised his hand. *"Bárufall."* His hand waves grew bigger and wilder on his story sea.

"Úveðr." The handcup ship rose, spun, and tipped.

"A storm?" I asked. I made the sound of thunder and wind, and made my fingers into rain.

He nodded. "Ahstoam!"

"A storm," I repeated. "Ho!" I called out to Ushag. "He was in a storm at sea!"

Our success had put heart back into the Northman, and he rose from his bed. Ushag tried to lead him back, but he only paced stiffly and muttered feverishly in his own talk. "He's done in. You shouldn't bother him," she whispered to me.

"He's not bothered," I said. "He's trying to tell us." The man listened closely to us, even coming right up to our faces to watch our lips move as we spoke. He towered over us, and was so pale he almost lit the dark byre with his own soft light. "He wants to tell us."

"He makes a body feel so small," whispered Ushag, peering up at him and standing as straight as she could. She put her hands on her hips and pointed back at the bed, but the man just made his hand ship and waves again, and he carried on.

He pointed into the little ship he'd made, touching it everywhere with the tip of his finger. *"Vegendr,"* he said. *"Vegendr. Vegendr."* He stood up straight and broad, giving us a fierce face and hacking at us with ghost sword and ax. Ushag frowned, and he hung his head.

"A ship of killers, that's plain enough," my aunt said, and spat into the straw. The man held out his hands, palms up, and spoke.

"No vegandi!" He played out the killing once more, shook his head, and hit his chest with his outspread hand. "Ulf," he repeated. He lifted the hair from his nape and pointed, and there was a cross inked in blue. *"Nei! No vega! Kristinn maðr."*

He had tears on his cheeks, trying to make us understand. He pressed his palms together. *"Kristinn.* Ahfarzher ooaht inevvan . . ." he said, and sat heavily, weakened by the effort. "Ahman."

He seemed to be suffering some type of Terror. We laid him back into his bed. "Well, I don't think he's a killer anymore, whatever he was before," I said, and patted his big, clammy hand.

"Ahman. Ahman," were his last words before he became insensible once more.

"No." Ushag watched him like you would a

strange dog: a strange dog with fine breeding and a shifty humor.

I woke the next day feeling stupid and ran straight-away to the byre. "Neen," I said, pointing at my chest. "Ushag," I added, pointing back at the roundhouse. "Breck." I slapped the cow's rump, and she frisked and protested. "Bo." I waved my hand at the heifer, and she came and leaned against me. The Northman's face lit up. He waited.

"Ulf," I said at last, pointing at him. He laughed.

"*Góð píka.* Nin, nin, nin. Ushah. Ushaaah." He repeated the names to himself.

"That'll do," I said.

Ushag brought in the food. "Ulf's his name," I told her. "And he might be wiggynagh, but he's also Christian."

"Oh, they've gone right up there, have they?" She piled his trencher high with leeks and colewort and took it to him. "Well, that's nothing to brag about here."

"Mister Ulf," she said, handing him his plate and looking him straight in the eye.

"Fru Ushah," he returned, and they shook hands. I've never seen two people more serious at a meeting.

"Come out now and help me salt the mackerel." She gathered all the nighttime simples into her box and waited for me on the threshold.

"No, I'm going to stay with Ulf." I filled my mouth with fish so that she could see any talk of mackerel salting, or anything else, was over. "I want to find out his story."

She nodded slowly and turned to go. "As useful as a blind tailor, as usual," she muttered as she went.

"Nin." After eating, he beckoned me to him. He'd cleared a space in the straw and chaff, and the smooth dirt showed through. Using his blade, he drew a ship of stick men in a stormy sea. All the men held weapons except the one with a cross hanging around his neck.

"Ulf," I said touching that one. Ulf nodded.

He got up from his bed, and he was wearing a garment of Ushag's; it was one of her longest tunics, but on him, it only fell to his thighs. He tried to pull it down over his bare legs, which I couldn't help noticing were covered in matted yellow hair. The tunic wouldn't do, so he wrapped himself in his rug. Then he squatted and scratched in the dirt again.

First, he drew a raid. The stick-men raiders coursed with wide-open mouths through a small village, where the people lay in the lanes and pathways stuck all over with blades. He drew children and old people, dogs, cats, and chickens without their heads, or without limbs, and all bleeding or weeping.

"*Úthlaup*," he said, indicating the entire scene.

"*Úthlaup*," I repeated. It was plainly a raid on some settlement somewhere.

He drew himself in his war weeds right in the middle of the killing, his weapon drawn, with a smile and a clenched fist. He shrugged at me sadly, and I nodded back. He had been one with the killers. He had been filled up with the bloodlust, just as they were.

Rubbing the dirt clear, he drew another raid, but this time the dead were all women and children. The raiders coursed as before, but this time the drawing showed Ulf at the center of the slaughter with his weapon at his feet and his hands hanging at his sides. Blood dripped from his fingertips. A dead woman at his feet was wearing the Christian's cross on a chain around her middle. The real Ulf groaned quietly.

"*Oh, iskald sál.*" He shivered. "*Blóð-sál.*"

I didn't know what those words meant, but he had the face of such sorrow on him and his body slumped so done in against the stall door that I held my breath. Bo leaned over and licked at his head, and that seemed to put some backbone into him, because he jumped and started acting out the storm at sea.

He reeled from side to side, making a thundering sound, and making lightning bolts with his hands and hurling them at me. The real Ulf shaded his eyes and pointed far away, and the story Ulf sighted an island on the horizon. The real Ulf crouched behind the feedbox, and the story Ulf hid from his crewmates in the stern. Once the storm had blown itself out and the crew were all busy with the aftermath, the story Ulf slipped over the side and set out to swim to the island.

Ulf pointed at the dead woman in his drawing, and at all the women and children in his scene, and put his hands to his heart as if it hurt him. He pointed at the raiders and, holding his belly as if he was sick, shook his head. He kept on shaking it as he slipped over the side and into a black night sea. In his story, it seemed to me that he was happy to drown rather than stay with his ship and the other raiders. Which happiness, in fact, he nearly won, because he no sooner left his ship than he was caught in the kelp forests that ring Carrick.

Kneeling in the dust, he formed the weed with his hands and arms. It tangled and knotted about his arms and legs. It caught in his hair and his mouth and left a slimy sweat everywhere it touched. Story Ulf fought and choked as long as he could, but in the end, the terrible weed beat him. He gasped for what he thought would be his last breath, and sank below the surface into the green world.

While he still had enough air in him to notice such things, he felt the brushing of smooth skin against his. Just as his air was leaving him, he felt the soft prodding of these bodies all alongside and under him. Just as he felt himself failing, a face with wild, black eyes rose to his own and bubbles tickled at his nose and mouth and encompassed him around. Then there was nothing until he woke to Ushag and me dragging him up the cliff path. "Sea girl," he said. "Sea girl." It seemed to be the only Carrick he knew, apart from his prayers.

Ulf's story had drawn in the day around us, and we sat in silence for some time. "Ushah?" he said, pointing at me. "Ushah *móðir*?" I didn't know what he meant. "Mamma?" he tried. "Ushah, mamma?"

"Oh, no." I got up as I heard Ushag and Ma come in with meat and drink. My voice rose. "No. Oh, no, no. Nin's mamma gone away." I puffed at my closed fingers and thumb and opened them, watching something light and precious fly away.

"Pff! Gone," I said. "And we don't know where." I mimicked losing something important. I looked inside the churn as if it might be there. "No mamma there," I said. I shaded my eyes and peered out the door. "Not there." I lifted Bo's tail and looked there. "No, not there. It's a mystery," I said. "A whole mother, gone entirely."

My aunt's face was a mask, but once again she couldn't meet my eyes.

"Auntie Ushag will tell you the story." I shrugged at Ulf, but he was watching Ushag with eyes as pale as the cave spiders.

"Well, then," she said at last to change the subject and all unsuspecting. "What's his story?"

She wasn't going to like it, but I couldn't help that. I took a deep breath. "Ulf was a raider, and he's been raiding around these parts with his people for years, but I think he killed some women and children when they were alone in their village one day, and also one was a Christian, and after that, he, well, I suppose he had a change of heart." I stopped and patted his shoulder. "Anyway, he doesn't want to be a killer anymore. He says he's a Christian man now."

"Is that right?" Ushag put the jug by his bed and waited for me to carry on. She raised her eyebrows at me.

"What?" I said.

"Nothing. How did he get into our net, then?"

There was no way out. I had to tell her the whole thing.

"Right," I said.

Ulf was watching closely.

"Well, here it is, and don't blame me. He said on the way back home, his ship was blown past Carrick in a storm, and he went overboard, and he tried to swim here but got himself tangled in the weed . . . in the sea forests . . . and he nearly drowned and . . . and then the merrows came and gave him air in bubbles and carried him into our net for us to find."

My aunt sat blinking at me like an owl. Her silence had grown. It used to be a quiet thing, but now it was loud and took up all the space between us. As soon as she came in, I could hear it. And there was something else too; I couldn't look straight at her face. There was something in it that ran my flesh cold. She looked like somebody thinking of doing an impossible thing just to see if she can, like turning inside out or flying to the sun. She looked reckless. She looked like somebody I didn't know.

Auntie Ushag sat rock still, and the sigh she breathed out seemed to come from some deep cave inside her body. She looked at me straight for the first time in weeks with her bright bird's eyes. They were the eyes of a person who'd had enough.

"Right," she said. "I've had it! Now I will tell you."

CHAPTER TEN

Ushag's Story

I CANNOT PRETEND ANY LONGER not to know what I know," sighed Ushag, and even Ulf could tell something was up. He turned his pale and freckled face to hers. "I'm done in from trying to keep it from you."

"Why have you, then?" I asked. "Why not just tell me?"

"You'll see." My aunt's voice dropped. "It's a hard story to tell . . . and to hear. It's not the sort of story you can tell a child.

"I'll have to go back somewhat, to the old Marreys. You've already heard from Scully and Ma, I'm sure, on how the family came to the cove"—Ma looked sheepish—"but now it's time for some truth. In the days when Merton was only a dozen families, the Marreys were driven out. Snug home and good living all lost, all at once and all because of a touch of the Scale.

"Well, I say good living . . . it had been that for generations, but there was a Hunger about, so the living wasn't as good as it had been. The fact is, even the oldest folk could remember only feasts as far back as memory took them. Somehow, through all the good years, they'd forgotten what it was to be hungry.

"The way I heard it from my father, most of Merton had some disfigurement in those days; there was one boy who lived a whole lifetime in just seven years, growing aged and feeble before he even reached his mother's shoulder. The southerners disagreed as to the nature of his Otherness, but everybody agreed it was unlucky for a child to age so contrary, and he was bound to bring trouble on them. Banishment was the cure, but the lad died before they could act, and his parents set for the mainland before the town could feel his loss. And they were right to do so, because a day later the mob burned everything belonging to that family."

Ushag fell silent, and I waited. My heart felt too big for my chest. She watched my face. "People do bad things when they're hungry," she said sadly.

"As it was with that boy, so it soon followed with the Marreys. As a girl, one of the grandmothers suffered terribly with the Scale. This was that grandmother called Tosha, a woman out of Strangers' Croft, and who was married to Doolish; she was shingled in thick sheets of Scale, and green and leaking they say it was too. Nobody had seen anything like it, and the family expected her to up and die at every moment. But she lived on, and given what they'd wanted to do to the aged boy, perhaps it's not so unexpected that soon Merton should turn on her. It didn't take long. In town she became known as the merrow wife, but she did not die of it, and the family did not run from the island.

"The Marreys just upped and took everything they could carry over Shipton-Cronk, and they came to the northernmost cove. We were always tight-knit, as close as snigs in a stream. There were two other brothers and a sister, all as yet unmarried and all now unlikely to be so. Nobody wanted to make a match with the family who boasted a merrow.

"At first they survived on salt and weeds, and sheltered in caves up the gorge. They found eels swarming in the rivers, and bats blackening the cave walls, and they ate them. They stole eggs from the nesting seabirds, and honey from the bees. And they found useful wreckage all along the shoreline — timbers curved and straight, all kinds of line and chain, anchor flukes, pinions, whiskey, blades, and boxes — all the flotsam of lives lost at sea, finding its way to Marrey Cove, where all this found stuff helped rebuild their lost lives.

"That first exiled generation built the roundhouse

from the loose stone and what all they found around the cliff and on the beach. Floundering ships spat out everything a body could want, and some things it could do without, such as French liquor or fish-nibbled bodies. In time, the house was filled with pallets and tables and pots and eating tools; filled with everything it needed to be a household. Those first cove Marreys never went back down south, being windy of its folk until the day they died, and that old scaly Tosha outlived the lot.

"Doolish and Tosha had seven children, of which five died and two lived: that being Monty Marrey and a sister. At twenty-three, sick of knowing only weather and loneliness, the sister was set for the mainland and left with a sailor out of Shipton.

"Being alone after the death of his parents, Monty Marrey sometimes went to Shipton to trade and drink. The Great Hunger had passed, and the folk who'd wanted to kill the aged child, the ones who'd driven his parents to the mainland and exiled the Marreys to the stormy cove, had grown old and died themselves. Everybody else was in the way of forgetting once more. They welcomed Monty as though he were a brother returned, and showed him the old hospitality whenever he went among them. In fact, in time he married a southerner — something unthinkable in the days of Doolish.

"It was Monty who started the stories to keep folk away from the cove." Ushag stopped now and pointed her finger at Ma, who turned away, red-faced, and fussed at Ulf's rug, pulling it right up over his nose and eyes and tucking him in so tight he started struggling. "Stories of sea monsters, and of unnatural things up the gorge," added Ushag. Ma poured a brew, spilled most of it, got up, turned around, reached for a cloth to wipe the mess, and, while reaching, spilled the rest. Ulf freed himself from under the rug and carefully took the cup from her hands.

"Denk yoo," he said, making a little bow to Ma, and went to sit by my aunt. He poured for her, and she took the cup and drank deeply.

"Thank you," she said.

"Folk were getting interested in the cove, and they kept coming up north to 'visit' Monty. I suppose he thought he had to do something. These visitors always went home again with a little something from the wreck hoards: a barrel of grog, or some like treasure. More and more of them came every time, until it was like living in the Michaelmas Fair and with people lugging boxes and bags of booty away with them. So down at the pub, Monty started telling them about Otherwise goings-on around our place: of having to fight savage merrow men for the body of some wrecked seaman he meant to decently bury, or of being caught in a terrible undertow dragged behind a giant white eel, or titans with uncountable legs and beaks and hooks opening up the sea itself from inside of—"

"From inside of giant whirlpools," I interrupted.

"Right." Ushag nodded.

Ma stood up. "Just because Monty Marrey lied about seeing such things, and you don't believe in them, doesn't mean they're not true," said Ma, and she crossed her arms and gave Ushag the stony eye.

"Well, never mind all that now. Sit down, Mureal. Rest yourself." Ushag patted the floor. Ma sighed and sat again. "It's all ancient history. Monty had his reasons for spreading the stories; I know it. Those wrecks turned up all sorts over the years. The family had lived close to the dirt for years, and sometimes something worth a trade at market turned up that made the difference between eating and empty bellies. Monty and the others who came later spread those stories all over, and they worked. In the end, nobody came to Marrey Cove without a Marrey on hand to guide them, and by my parents' time, folk had stopped coming altogether.

"Monty married, and his wife, Creena, had five children, of which two died and three lived, and one of them that lived was my father, Hugo. My mother, a Shipton woman called Jinn, added the cow byre and traded for a cow and some hens. Those from Shipton are ever looking to their purses. They have a feel for buying and selling, and my mother was no idler in that; she ruled the wreck hoard and drove hard bargains for it down south. My father was a healer, as his mother had been, and he passed it to me.

"I was born into a family of six girls, of which all lived, but not for long. First, there was your mother, and then Edder, and then me, and then the three littlest ones.

"There was a new Hunger about when I was a child, and this time the Little Brothers were calling it the Last Hunger, as if they knew something we didn't. There were rumors from the mainland of people roasting rats, and of mothers eating their own babies. Edder was sent away with the missionary women, and though my father was sickened to do so, it saved her, for the other three just withered away until they were nothing but bellies on sticks, and they were dead by seven years.

"There being no boy, in time Ven was to take on our household. She was three years older than me, and didn't I just think her the bright, shining one!" Ushag gave me a quick, shy smile. I'd never heard her speak such words, or seen a face such as the face on my aunt at that moment; she looked like a white dove had risen right in front of her and called her by name. She looked like the moon had started to sing a lullaby. She looked young. "My sister was a great one for stories, both the Old ones and those from her own fancy . . ." She looked like she felt foolish. "And I hung on her words."

"She told stories?" It was a shiny tidbit. But I didn't know this Ushag. "And you hung on her words?"

Ma rubbed her knees and enjoyed a burst of laughter. In the silence that followed, Scully stretched and grinned up into the roof and Ulf raised his eyebrows at me. I shook my head, and Ushag quietly carried on.

"I was born into this place, and for years I knew nothing but sea, rock, hunger, work. Hunger, rock, work, sea — and the girl. Not you. The other girl: my sister. Ven. She was a honey-tongue. Her stories and all her foolishness were to me as real as my father's cures. I spent my days collecting for the Herbal, and drying and steeping and storing, and my evenings listening to my sister talk. I wanted nothing more from life than to live here with Father and Ven and to be let alone forever. I never wanted to marry. You won't believe me, and I don't care if you do, but I doted on her.

"Even as a small girl, Ven was always a big one for love. Mothers and their children, clans and their kings, animals and their masters; she liked all the stories of love, but those about the love between men and women were her favorites. We played at love lost and love found, shimmer-white ladies saving or being saved by cursed lords in the forms of beasts, and weddings and vows and suchlike. We played at her stories for days at a time, with me always the enthralled knight, the enchanted tree, the talking well, or the wicked ice hag, while she was always the sweet girl who had to do nothing but lie about in bowers, waiting to be loved."

I couldn't have been more surprised if my aunt had told me she used to make lace, or compose poems. I suppose my face showed it, because she laughed. "I didn't mind. She was the sweet girl. I was happy to play at the hero—or the villain or the tree—or any other part her stories needed.

"Then my mother died. I was nine. Ven was thirteen. We buried her down at the monastery, due to her changing her mind about that god at the last moment. My father wouldn't come to the church, but he put on a wake in her honor that night, at which they drank all the whiskey from a whole year's wrecking, and the fiddler was found three days later, senseless in Strangers' Croft, still stinking of it.

"Ven took to rambling then. She rambled all the way down to Merton, and naturally enough, soon she was in love. She took to Colm Breda like he was pudding, and that was it for our plays and stories. She was too old for them now, and for me. I looked out for her, but she was always elsewhere with him. When she was home, she spent most of her time at the well, gazing at herself in the water and putting her hair this way or that, rubbing lemon juice into her shoulder skin, or making herself a bosom by squashing her chest upward into her tunic. She told me to leave her alone. She told me to go away. Then she stopped talking to me and only rolled her eyes when I said we should play.

"Anyway.

"Father said we'd need a man about our place after he'd gone, and he set to bargaining with the Bredas for Colm to come and live with us in the cove instead of Ven going to Merton. Him being the youngest and them having a wild crew of all boys, it wasn't such a hard bargain to drive. Ven and Colm were wed when she was fourteen—and then you were born. Father died while she was carrying you, but he knew you to be a woman-child and spent much time with his hand on her belly, feeling you move. He died with you quickening in the womb under his hand." Ushag stopped and took another drink. She wasn't used to talking so much and so long; her voice cracked as she went on, though her face was pinker and her eyes brighter than I'd seen for a long time. Those memories were sad, but it seemed to make her happy to talk about them. "You were born under the same star as your mother, and she passed her Scale to you, along with your face and your stories."

"My mother had the Scale too?" I felt the heat start to prickle up my neck.

"I told you that," said Ushag.

"No. You didn't!" I replied. She looked at me with her head tilted.

"Yes, I did." She looked away. "You've forgotten."

As if I'd forget. I clamped my lips tight. I didn't want to say anything that would make her stop.

"Ven's was a bit worse than yours and sometimes bled. Our father taught me to tend to it. Nobody down south had a word to say about it until the Christians started up about their Doom. Then all of a sudden, she was a monster. It was a bad time in Carrick — and the entire world, if you listened to the priests. The Brothers told everybody that the end of the world was coming and that, if we didn't join up in time, we were all to burn and bleed and break our bones in their hell just for being born. We Marreys all gave them the deaf ear, and I suppose we were lucky to be so away from it all, but there were plenty down south to listen . . . and not just listen but adorn the story with all their own frights and shambles. Well, you heard the Father just the other day going on about all the signs from their god. Sometimes I wonder if the Brothers live in the same world as I do." She drained her mug and poured another.

"So everybody was in a right terror, and down

south my sister and her scaly baby became another sign. She was followed and cursed in the streets. She was pelted by some, at the markets and in the pub. When a turnip hit you square in the head, she stopped going anywhere and stayed only with Colm and me at home. People do bad things when they're fearful."

"She even stopped coming up the moaney, though I told her the Scale proved her kinship to the life of the sea and she should be proud." Ma stroked my head. "And her daughter, too."

"Mmm," said my aunt.

"After your pa died, she took to rambling again, as I've said before. It was her way. This time, though, she walked, and walked and walked until she wasted away from it. In time she walked her way down south again, where folk took their chance to prove themselves to the town's new god. I've never heard such bile-talk as that which she told me they spat at her.

"They said Colm had been cursed by his marriage to her. They said as how he'd gotten a taste for cold-blooded flesh from touching her scaly skin, but she was now not salty enough for him. They asked if her young husband had gone to a merrow lover, and some even made a song of it. They said he'd been disgusted by her half-bloodedness and he wanted a full merrow wife, and that he drowned trying to get himself one. They said she had killed him as sure as if she'd held his head underwater herself. She had killed him by loving and wedding him with the merrow curse on her, and she only had herself to blame for the whole sorry mess."

Ushag was finding it harder and harder to carry on and stopped to drink again. Her eyes were dry, but they looked to be burning in her head. I felt a coldness rise in me against the southerners and the priests. I held my scaly arm to the rush light and wondered how such a small thing could cause such trouble. "Ven knew old Monty had started those stories about the north cove merrows, as all us Marreys did. And she knew why, too, but after all her suffering, I think she started to believe in them," added Ushag. "She was always too easily fooled by a good story."

We all sat in silence and thought of Ven.

"She couldn't really have believed all that about her being to blame for Pa?" I said. Ma and Ushag swapped a look. Scully sighed and started to pick at his fiddle strings. Their strange twanging and popping filled the cow byre.

"You mean like somebody believing in stories about drowned fathers marrying merrows, or missing mams living like salamanders in caves?" Ushag got up and walked to the door. "I should finish that mackerel, and get on with the gutting," she said quietly, rubbing at her brow. A basket of reeds and rushes by the door caught her eye. "I should start that dipping. I should . . ." She looked about and saw the jug and cups. "I should get on . . ."

Ma took her hand. "You should finish telling it, Birdie," she said. "Now you've started." Ushag pressed her fingers to her eyes. A fat unexpected tear rolled down her cheek. It left a clear track in the grime and soot, and I was left dumbstruck.

"People do bad things when they're hopeless," she said. "Not because they want to or because they are bad people. They think something must be done—and so they go ahead and do something. That's what happened to Ven.

"One day I went bagging up the gorge and left you with your mother. She'd been so harrowed by the talk, it hurt just to look into her eyes, but this day she seemed brighter, and so I left you with her. She said she was going to make a moon pie." My aunt choked, and her voice grew tight. She swallowed over and over as if trying to keep something down. "I came back by the cliff path and I saw her and I knew straightaway what she was doing, but I couldn't stop her. You were up the beach, playing. I was wondering why she'd left you there alone. Then from the cliff path I saw her . . . I saw her walk into the water. She just walked into the water." I didn't like where this story was traveling. "It was a high tide such as I'd never seen, and you know the undertows breed like longtails in those heavy tides. It was too late.

"She looked back at you once, and then kept walking. She just kept walking." Ushag's voice broke and her tears fell, but I was like dusty ground—dry and hard. Ma rose and went to my aunt. She bent and touched her face, dabbing at the dropping tears and blowing gently over the hot eyes. Ushag rubbed at her face like the tears were dirty. I felt nothing.

I just had to sit there and let her finish her story; that's all I had to do.

"She walked into the sea. Her shawl opened all around her in the water. She took off her belt and tunic, and they all floated away in one of the smaller tows. Then she was bare except for her wedding earrings, the great silver hoops Colm had gotten as her wedding token, and that she herself had put the holes in her ears to take. She walked into the sea until it passed over her entirely: over her shoulders, over her chin, over her mouth and nose, until only her eyes stayed above the water. Her hair encompassed her, spread out all around, waving like black weed in the green water and floating on the surface even after her head had gone under. I shouted once with all my voice, all the voice I could find inside me, and the shout rang all around the cove. She didn't hear me.

That's when I dropped the eels and started running. I knew what she was doing.

"When I looked next, she was gone.

"From that tall cliff, I jumped in. I had no fear of the fall, no fear of the rocks, no fear of the tows. I dived and swam and searched the kelp, and even went back with nets, but she was gone. The undertows had taken her. As she knew they would." Ushag stopped at last. Ulf tried putting his hand on her shoulder, but her tears had gone as quickly as they had come, and she shrugged his hand away. "Love, eh?" she finally said to Ma, who nodded and sucked furiously at her pipe. My aunt and I sat back and looked at each other with eyes like strange cats.

Ushag leaned forward. "Happy now?" she said.

CHAPTER ELEVEN

Wreckage

I WASN'T FIT TO BE AROUND. Honor Bright, this time Auntie Ushag didn't have to tell me to go away; I didn't want to do anything else. Why should she tell me such a story? Was she so sick of my questioning her that she just wanted to finish it once and for all? Because plainly when somebody's dead, any story about them is likewise. Was she jealous of her lost sister? Did she want to sicken me of stories entirely? Ushag's terrible silence had now settled on me.

I needed to think. I felt like I might turn inside out from all the traveling storms within me. Before she could say anything else, I left our place and went straightaway to the cove. Today was a day for the cool, unchanging sea if ever I knew one.

I grabbed my stone sack and marched into the water. It was fresh and clean, and I wanted to drink it, to scour the sound of my aunt's voice from my ears, to clear the taste of this story from my mouth and flush it out of me in a Flux. I pushed my legs hard against the currents and, open-eyed, sank straight to the seabed. I sat before the kelp forest, and I dwelled on Ushag's story, and on Mam.

I thought I remembered that day on the beach, but was I really remembering the sea and my mother's face? Did I truly remember her turning back to smile as she waded out and away from me? Or was I now just remembering the story of it?

I looked upward and pictured how it might have been to sink forever into this dappling light, how its air would rise as the body sank, falling slowly, face to the sky and all above just hair and bubbles. Considering how I felt when I was getting breathless—how some force pushed me to the surface and a good fresh lungful—to think of somebody falling back willingly into the dark element gave me sad chills all through.

In my mind's eye, I saw Mam floating downward and her body settling soft and pink upon the grit and shells. She surged quietly on the tide. Her fingers and toes waved like anemones and swelled like the puffers. A cloud of tiny silver fish swam over her head, and she stared upward through them, giving me the morbid and pitiful eye. I couldn't help seeing it—in spite of not quite believing it.

Because she would never have done that. I knew it, I just knew.

Mam was happy-natured and bright, Ushag said so herself. She was to take over the household at her father's death, so she must have been a sensible sort of person too. She walked Carrick alone for a year after Pa died, so she must have been brave. And she was patient; Ma said so. She was good at just sitting through troubles until they were over. A bright, brave, sensible, and patient person wouldn't do that terrible thing. She couldn't have. I just knew it.

A sea otter gliding through the kelp fixed its eye on the urchin herds grazing at the edges of the forest. Picking one out, it rolled onto its back and rested the spiky thing on its belly as it swam. It gripped a rock in one sweet-looking paw and bashed the urchin until the water filled with blood all around, and then it carried it to the surface to eat.

The kelp seemed to reach out for me with its clinging wrack and stingers. The awful undertow hid itself in there, and I could hear it forever rushing on, pouring toward the future, and wanting to drag me with it. I let go of the stone sack and rose to the sun, breathing again. Deep, long breaths. I breathed like this all the way up the cliff path.

Back at home, in spite of her recent tears, my aunt was all high spirits. Ulf was out of the byre and sat by our hearth dressed in what looked to be a set of tapestries and a pearl hat. The corner trunk was open. He waved a mug at me as I came in. "Ho! Nin," he greeted me. The pot was full and on the fire; I couldn't help noticing that it smelled better than it had for some time. Neither of them talked, but the house still rang with cheerfulness and a sort of fellow feeling. The fire crackled, the pot bubbled, and our North-man hummed bits of airs and parts of tunes, which Ushag joined in now and then. The mead jug sat by the hearth, almost empty. A fresh one waited nearby.

"All right?" My aunt glanced at me and handed me a stew.

"Suppose so," I said, tucking in. I ate for a while and then said quietly with a full mouth, "Except obviously I don't believe it."

Propped like a standing stone with Ulf's stew in her hand, Ushag's face fell. She raised one eyebrow. "Don't believe what?" She handed him the trencher.

"Don't believe what you said about Mam." I let it sink in. "How do you know that she was . . . you know? Drowning herself."

"I know it because I saw it." She sat and served herself while giving me the full show of tutting, rais-ing her eyes to heaven, and shaking her head. I didn't let on I saw any of it. I wanted to have this out to its end, wherever that was.

"You don't know," I said. "All you saw was that she walked into the water."

"I saw what I saw."

"You saw her walk into the water . . ."

"That's right." Ushag poured herself another brew.

"And then you settled for yourself that she'd drowned herself," I finished.

My aunt looked bothered. Ulf was following the talk closely while spooning stew into his mouth. He stopped for a moment to search about the hearth for something.

"I did not decide. I saw," insisted my aunt, finding and handing the salt bowl to him.

"Denk yoo," he said.

"You saw her walk into the water. You didn't see her drown."

"Heishan! You talk like the priest," she snapped. "Slippery as a greased pig."

"There's no point in being rude," I said, and I meant it truly, but Ushag sat back on her heels and hissed at me through her teeth. Ulf hardly put his spoon down by his empty trencher before she filled it again, slopping stew all about him as she did so. She also slammed him down another brew.

"Denk yoo. Denk yoo," he said, and smiled into his mug as he drank.

"I saw her." Ushag was stubborn. "I know."

"I know," I said. "I know what you think you saw. But you're wrong."

"You *know*." She was shouting now. "How can you know anything? You were only three. You never knew her."

"No, but I know myself. And I know I'm just like her. You told me so." Ushag lowered her eyes. "And I know that she would never do that thing."

There was a silence I couldn't read. Ushag took me suddenly by the shoulders and studied my face with something that looked like love in spite of her curses.

"Spit hag! You *are* like her. She also took no mind of the real world and its regular folk. She had her Scale; it made her special." She shook me a bit, but not hard. "And she, too, ran to the sea whenever there was trouble, or any hard thing, to be dealt with."

"What does that mean?" A cold stone had settled in my belly.

"It means that when trouble came, as it always does, she only had her stories and the sea to help her." The stone had risen into my throat. "Those of us who weren't special just had to get on with it. She didn't. She gave up."

Now the heat in my throat and the cold in my belly met, and a storm rolled right into the middle of my chest. I wanted to walk out of there and never come back. "Why are you telling me all this now?" I asked my aunt.

"Because you asked. And you asked. And you keep on asking," said Ushag. "And because you are so like her..." she added almost in a whisper and with a groan.

I knew what she was thinking then. She thought I would do it too, the thing she thought Ven had done. I stood up. "Well, and because I'm so like her, I can tell you that what you thought you saw—you didn't!" I had never bellowed like that in my life. "I would never do that, so you needn't trouble yourself about me—and neither would my mother. She didn't just walk away or drown herself. She just went home to her real family. And I don't blame her! Why would she want to stay with you?" Startled, Ulf jumped to his feet, and my aunt leaned away from me. Not for long, though. She crossed her arms against me, and her voice was cold.

"Well. There we are. You asked, and I told." She turned her back to me and, unasked, filled Ulf's mug once more. He held the mug in both hands to his chest and watched us. The merrow on his hand flickered in the firelight. "Now it's your story as well as mine. You must do with it as you see fit. As I have had to." Ulf and Ushag's eyes met over the mug. His eyes were soft, even beyond that silly softness caused by a few brews, but she met them with ice and gravel and turned back to me with a closed face. "I'm done," she said, and got up and left. The room's cheer melted away.

"Orraht, Nin?" Ulf asked me.

"I suppose so."

"*Gott,*" he said, and taking a third helping and the jug with him, he followed my aunt outside. I was left alone by the fire. My heart thundered, black clouds filled my head, and the lightning shot through me like shock eels. My aunt had fixed her sister in the worst of stories, and I was going to have to find another way to get her to open her mind and see the truth. In this humor, I went to my bed.

I dreamed I swam again in the kelp forest. In tangled light and flowing undertow, a wrecked hull rocked white and skeletal in the long grass. Its keel, ribs, and battens were marked all over with hands sinuous, like anemones, and right in its middle sat an ornate locked trunk. I opened it, and the water around me filled at once with pearls, all floating upward. I grabbed at one as it rose and brought it to my face. I saw the kraken inside with all its hooked legs; another held a line of people with torches walking forever along undersea paths; another, a wailing changeling child. I woke up. I had a feeling of doom.

Words weren't working. They weren't proof. I was going to have to take my aunt to see for herself, even if I had to drag her.

CHAPTER TWELVE

Cave of Hands

I WOKE AT DAWN, BUT AUNTIE USHAG was still up before me, cutting and dipping rushes. We're lucky to have the grove of bees just up behind us; Ma and Scully burn tallow for light and have to live with the stink of it — it's like the back of the butcher's after a hot day. Beeswax burns clean and sweet, and I've heard that the Brothers even have rules about it, such as it's only to be used by the highest of their priests, but my aunt says that's the kind of rule just made to be broken.

She'd already stripped and cut the bundle, and was now warming the beeswax. The morning washed in pearly and calm; even Ushag moved slowly at her work. I went and sat by her.

"Put your clothes on," she said. I fetched my tunic. "You're too old to get about like that anymore." She gave me a handful of rushes. "And Ulf is here now."

"Ulf," I said.

She couldn't help herself. Her lips twitched and pressed together in a tight grin. She reddened.

"Will you wed with him?" I asked.

Her grin vanished, and she looked at me straight and steady. "I will never marry," she said in such a way as I knew it to be true.

We stripped the rushes for a while in the cool before the day got up. My aunt was in a milder humor than she had been all summer. The night before seemed forgotten. I slipped a close look at her face. Perhaps it was. She had drunk a lot. There were even small, friendly smiles between us.

"I want you to come up the gorge with me," I said, on the strength of the change.

"When?" she asked.

"Today." I watched her struggle not to ask me what for. "There's a giant eel landlocked in a cave up there," I told her, and showed its measure with my hands. I held them as apart as they'd stretch.

Her face lit up somewhat; she never lets go a chance to fill the pot. "Well, it should be all right." I waited while she thought some more, and then she clinched it. "I suppose so," she said.

As we left the yard, a warm, salty breeze lifted the corners of the eel bag and played with our hair. After our weeks of stillness, this little wind cheered us no end, and when we reached the shore, even Ushag was sprightly in her step. On the beach it strengthened, and we had to lean into it to stay upright; at the mouth of the gorge, it was pushing at us from behind, and we kept breaking into helpless canters and trots upon its back. We couldn't help it. Even my aunt was laughing and whooping as we were buffeted into and up the gorge.

There was some change come over Auntie Ushag since yesterday, since she told about her and Ven. She seemed smoothed somehow; in spite of the terrible story, her movements were more of a piece, her speech softer, her face more open. Already a grin and two bursts of laughter this morning, and she was meeting my eyes with no sliding or slipperiness. I didn't know why she was so good-natured all of a sudden, but I was counting on it to get us through what I had to show her.

Ushag led us along the stony river for a while, and then turned onto a path running under an overhanging ledge and hidden by creepers and fern. This sheltered path was just tall enough for a small person to stand up and walk along. It saved us some time splashing and clambering up the river. Watching my aunt ahead of me, she seemed a goat or some other rough, skillful beast. Neither slowing nor quickening, her feet just kept plodding on through the green light of the overhang. This was plainly her own shortcut that she knew well; it struck me that perhaps she and Ven had used it.

We reached the place of the carvings. The tremblings had shaken the cliffs, and rocks had fallen into the chasm, closing some openings and opening others. Some of the stones lay on the ground now, their figures broken up and scattered. Others were still standing, although the openings they marked were all changed. I spotted the deep-cut spiral stone that marked the cave of hands. The entrance was smaller, but there was still enough room to crawl.

"There," I said, and we shuffled inside on our knees.

The merrows started up as soon as we touched the darkness, just as we could stand up again. The song traveled along rocky steeps in the cliff's belly and flowed into all its gaps and passages. It sang into our ears and down through the hallways of our bodies until it filled our hearts with all its lonely wilderness. Ushag was shaken, I could tell. She flattened herself against the wall, and her sweat gleamed in the dark light.

"All right?" I said.

"I suppose so," she replied, but I could see she wasn't. "Where's this eel, then?"

I took her hand and led her to the dark pool. Words not working so well between her and me these days, I didn't want to tell her about the hand marks; I wanted her to find them for herself. So I stepped back and left her to it. It didn't take long. I heard her murmuring.

"What?" I said.

"Come here." Her voice sounded angry, but when I moved closer and could see her face better, I saw she was only baffled. "Is this what you really brought me up here to see?"

I nodded.

"Well?" I asked.

"Well, what?" she said.

"Have you seen this before?" I asked.

"Not really," she answered.

"Well, have you or haven't you?" I couldn't take any more of this foggy, circling talk. My aunt gave me a sharp eye and stood up as if to leave. "I'm sorry. I'm sorry," I said. She couldn't leave now. I pulled at her hands. "Please?" She knelt again. "Have you seen them before?"

"I have seen hand marks like these, but it was down south and a long time ago. They were on the cliff near the harbor, and the men had found them long before me. They'd drawn all over them and . . ." She glanced at me and stopped.

"Go on," I said.

"Well," she carried on. "All right. They'd turned

them into figures of women. It was hard to see what they'd been before the . . . additions."

Ushag bent to look closer. She followed the cloud of hand marks as they drifted down the rock wall. Near the ground she found the small webbed hands and squatted by them for some time. She did what I'd done and put her hand into the hand mark. It matched in every singularity but the webbing. Still touching it, Ushag spoke.

"I heard that the Old ones used to do this," she said softly. "I've seen markings like those outside. The shapes and such. They're all over Carrick. I've seen pictures in the caves by Merton, and up by Strangers' Croft. Mostly fish."

"Were any of those markings like these?" I had a feeling my aunt would just keep talking about everything but the point if I let her. I had to ask. I had to finish it. "Were they webbed?" I asked.

"No," said Auntie Ushag. She put her hand on my shoulder, and we looked at the wall together. "They weren't webbed." The merrow song had faded and seemed to be now just one lone voice wailing somewhere far away. My aunt slid her hand down my arm and stroked my Scale. She was trembling.

"I don't know," she said, and her voice became a groan as she talked. "I don't know. I don't know."

This sounded to me like the start of a conversation,

a real conversation, but before I could say a word, Ushag tore off her tunic and jumped into the dark pool. For a moment I thought she'd run mad and was trying to drown herself in the waist-deep water. She was thrashing about with both arms under the surface. "Bag!" she shouted. "Bag!"

I grabbed the eel bag and pushed it down into the pool. I had thought the cave cold and had been starting to shiver, but that black water changed my mind. It seemed to cut through the flesh and freeze the very blood of my hands. And there was Auntie Ushag crashing about in it up to her waist and her arms right under, holding something down there.

I opened the bag's mouth. "Ho!" I called to her. Under the water, all was writhing parts, and I couldn't tell slimy eel from slippery arms and legs. Ushag wrestled something into the bag, something with length and girth and icy vigor. With a swing of her arm and a twist of her hand then, the bag was tied and on the ground, where it lay struggling and twisting.

Panting, Ushag gripped my shoulder with a wet, cold hand and laughed. She made as if to pull me in with her, but lost her footing and went under. Her feet appeared, like she'd stood on her head down there, and then disappeared as she righted herself.

"There's a tunnel," she said. "Right down the bottom, there's a tunnel."

"So?"

"So I saw a tunnel. It's not long. There's light at the end."

I watched her face show all the marks of excitement. She bobbed up and down in the water to keep from freezing. She grabbed me and pulled.

"I don't know what's the matter with you. It's a tunnel," she said as if that was all there was to it. She pulled at me again, and at once I was in the dark pool with her.

My breath was knocked from my chest, and I believe my mind left my body for a moment too. I had never known such cold. Even snow was warmer. Within moments, countless blades pricked at my feet and hands, and in a few moments more, the blades were stabbing.

"What! Whaaat?" My brain and teeth hurt so much, I was worried I would die from it. Auntie Ushag shook me and softly slapped at me until that was worse than the cold. "All right!" I said. "All right!" She slapped at me once more for fun. "Stop it!" She did and grinned.

"You're a delicate lady now, you are." She laughed, poking me until I had to grab her finger and twist it. "Tender. And. Fair."

"It's all very well for you," I said through chattering teeth. "With your leathery old hide. You feel nothing. But just you remember—I am a shy wood violet, and you should treat me so." I started laughing and so did she, but as usual I couldn't stop, and soon the waves of tears broke. I fought to master my flushes and tics and sobs. It was like I had become somebody else: somebody with no sense at all. Then as quickly as it came, it was gone, and I didn't know how to feel again. Except that I was to freeze to death if I didn't do something quickly.

We stood dripping side by side for a moment in the dark and cold. Ushag took my hand, and I couldn't help noticing that hers didn't shake at all. I was a chattering mass of bones and teeth from the marrow out.

"Coming?" she invited me, and disappeared entirely under the black water.

"I suppose so," I said, and the water slammed shut over my head.

CHAPTER THIRTEEN

Salamander

AUNTIE USHAG'S PALE SOLES KICKED above black water for a moment and disappeared down into the pool. I followed her just in time. In a moment she'd gone, leaving only a faint trail that melted away almost as fast as I tracked it downward. A tunnel cut through the rock wall, filled now only with bubbles and my aunt's silvery wake. Telling my pounding heart that it would all be all right, I kicked after her.

My bones were aching from cold, and in spite of it being only a short journey, I was tortured all its way by the thought of being buried alive inside the cliff. It was a tight fit, that tunnel, and would've made a chilly tomb. Wriggling, rolling, now serpentine, now otter-like, and somewhat harrowed by sharp points in the rock and the feeling I would run out of air, I pulled myself along hand over hand and made a bee-line for the light. Near its mouth, the tunnel and the rock pressed in. I was gripped at the shoulders and pinned for one panicked moment, and then Ushag's hand reached into the dark, grabbed mine, and pulled.

I slipped from that tunnel like a hare from its coat. "Snug, eh?" said my aunt. She wrung the water from her hair and shook herself like a wet dog. Her skin was like a plucked hen all over, and her lips were blue.

I stood shivering, knee-deep in another pool in another, more sizable cave. This one was sandy-floored, and filled with greenish light from a gap in the cliff at its sea end. Through it I could see dangling vines and a line of white sand, and the sea foaming. Waves surged back and forth through the gap, pushing halfway up into the sea cave before pulling back. I stepped out of the pool into thick sand.

Straightaway my feet started to burn; not burn like fire but like some of Ushag's cures. I hopped back and forth between feet a little. "It's the salt," said my aunt, tasting the sand. I looked about. Every pinnacle and mound was shining in its cap of salt. The cliff's insides towered above us in strips of red, pink, grey, and black, and everywhere my eyes met stone mounts and steeps, boulders and their shadows. It was as I fancied a castle might be, with its turrets and pillars and such, though a ruined, pockmarked sort. The walls were hived with cells; the monks could've moved right in. Just above my head, broad rock shelves angled back into the shadow, and the roof seemed carved out with juts and slabs like stone wings and altars.

I went to the sea cave's edge, where the salty burning seemed less. Where the wall met the sandy ground, a pit fell away into the deep earth and a terrible stink rose. Kneeling to see better, I soon wished I hadn't. It was full to the brim with dead beasts: both those recently dead and those that were only bones, and some that were in between. Gazing into that pit, I saw how a person might survive in these caves after all; somebody who was beyond caring, that is, and toughened into a hard life. Not somebody used to a warm hearth and decent food. I noticed all around me hallways leading deep into the cliff.

It would be a cold life, and filled with hunger, but I saw how people might believe in stories of cave dwelling. It wouldn't be impossible. You could eat from the pit if you had to.

"Come and see this," called Auntie Ushag from the other side of the cave. I made a dash across the salt and found her by another pit. This one held quite a hoard. There were burnt timbers, old barrels and staves and rims, charcoal, blades and handles, nets and buoys, and among it all, countless old shoes that had rotted and turned green. I hopped from foot to bare, stinging foot. "One of life's little jokes."

Ushag laughed, poking at all the once-fine leathers, the toggles, the buckles and pearl buttons. They fell apart.

"Funny," I said and pointed at it all. "What is it?"

"It's a wreck pit," my aunt said, picking out of it a blackened kettle.

I knelt down. "And what's that?" I pointed at a string of bones curling away from the pit and under the sand. Auntie Ushag shrugged.

"Could be anything," she said, still poking about in the wreck pit for anything useful. "Looks like a tailbone."

I followed the tailbone with my hand; it was long and snaky and spiraled back over itself several times. Brushing the sand away as I followed its length, and fully expecting a serpent or eel or some such thing, I was taken aback to come across leg bones, and then a pair of hips. I don't know what I was thinking exactly, but the sight of those legs, and their tail, robbed me of words. I dug now with some purpose I wouldn't confess even to myself.

I uncovered a bleached backbone, and then a set of sturdy ribs. At the top of the ribs, some broken bones fell away into the sand. They were almost buried, but I could see what they were. Arms. Softly, I scraped the sand away, following the bones; a neck, short and thick, appeared. Feeling light-headed, I stopped digging. The skeleton stretched before me now.

A small split at the tail's tip caught my eye. The tail wound itself in spirals for a good measure; then the shortish, bowed leg bones splayed out from the hips. There was the backbone and the fine ribs and, farther up still, the arms and neck.

Ushag came to my side as I sat blinking and breathing. "What is it?" she asked.

I couldn't answer her. I couldn't talk. I reached out and scooped handfuls of sand away from the neck and head. A jaw appeared, partly broken and lost, then the rest of a broad, heavy skull with sizable eyeholes. It had plainly been a head of singular ugliness. My aunt and I were struck both quiet and still by it.

"What is it?" she asked again.

I still couldn't talk. We stared. I put my hand to the jaw, and it fell apart entirely. Drawing a line in the sand around the bones, I fleshed the creature out, so to speak, and when I was done, we both stood back and stared some more.

A creature with a human-like body and a long eel-like tail revealed itself. I could see where the heart might fit, and the guts, liver, and lights. In my mind's eye, the bones clad themselves in shimmering scales, and somewhere deep inside me, a great relief shimmered also, and spread. As it did so, the relief became a calm, and then a victory. Not a proud victory, but a glad one. Ushag, meanwhile, had turned the grey of mealy flour. "Is it?" she hissed.

"I suppose it must be," I said, and she took my arm and sat down suddenly.

"Salt," I reminded her, and she stood again. She had to lean against the cave wall; the shock had made her light-headed. I watched her struggle to make sense of what we were seeing, and I'm ashamed to confess I took some pleasure from it. For once, it was good not to be the only one who didn't know what to think.

Her face fell prey to every type of tremble, and went from red to grey and back again several times, but her eyes stayed fixed on the bones. I could see her thinking; her eyes had become all rules and measures. "I suppose it must be," she whispered to herself. Then she covered her face, and when she showed herself again, she was laughing and crying at once. "I suppose so," she repeated, and she put her arm around my shoulder and pulled me to her.

We stood quietly for a while.

Auntie Ushag touched the merrow bones with her toes. They clattered softly. "It must've been a male," she said, and it was strange to hear her talking about it like that; as if she believed. "Look at its tail."

"And its head," I whispered, somewhat disgusted. It was a very big head, and from the size of the holes, the eyeballs must have been as big as turnips. My aunt laughed, but high-pitched and hard, and I could see she was all-of-a-heap. I rubbed her shaking hands in mine.

"It's smaller than you'd think, isn't it?" she said faintly. "Although, you know, truly how big is a merrow?"

"They're merrow bones," I said. "They are."

She nodded up at me. "I know."

"And where there's merrow bones . . ." I went on carefully. She nodded again but was looking more and more worried with every moment. "There's bound to be merrows." I thought perhaps she hadn't put together all the proof; that she hadn't seen yet what it all meant.

"And if the merrows are real—" I started, but before I could go on, she butted in.

"Ven could be one," she finished. "No need to go on and on about it!"

"Well, that's all I'm saying," I said.

Now she was seeing what I saw. If the story was true, then Mam could be still alive out there in the sea—living her fishy life and watching me grow. My Other mother, sending gifts in from the wrecks to our cove, singing to us and paying court to the kraken on our behalf. My aunt clenched her open hands onto her knees and started rocking to and fro. She was making a pent-up sort of noise.

What was the matter with the woman? She never behaved like this. I'd never even seen her cry until these last few days, and she surely never moaned or groaned or any of that business, even when she had the toothache. Even when our last cow, Kecky, died of a pox, she just butchered it for the eating, saying it was pointless to have a whole clutch of feelings about such things as dead cows. "You can howl and leak all you like," she'd said. "But when you're done, the lost thing's still lost, and the dead are still dead." And she loved that cow.

Now here she was, moaning and rocking, leaking like an old bucket.

"It's not Mam!" I said, thinking this might be why she was so troubled. "It's male—and it's too small. Mam was a fully grown woman and would've made a fully grown merrow." Auntie Ushag kept right on weeping.

After a while she started to ruin my victory. I felt it dribbling out of me.

"All right?" I asked her at last.

"Oh, well." She sniffed. "You know."

I waited.

"The thing is . . ." she started. "The thing is, you

know how the southerners tormented your mam and drove her back up here to us?"

"Yes," I said.

"Well, the thing is, Neen . . ." She swallowed heavily. "The thing is the southerners weren't the only ones." She covered her face. "I did it too. I said things. Things such as a sister should never say."

So what? I thought at the time. *What's a bit of fighting between sisters?* I'd seen enough of brothers and sisters in Shipton to know they weren't always a shining dream of kinship.

"When they drove her out of town, we should've been kind, but I was . . . I was so angry when she'd gone off down south and come back with Colm," she told me, and hung her head. "I was nothing to her after he came. She only wanted him then, and her games and stories were all for him. My father saw and made me treat her Scale without him. He said it was the sort of thing a sister did best, and could prove to be the cure for my anger, too. But I'd tell her there wasn't much could be done for her and, in time, her Scale would most likely spread. I told her that Colm would most likely not stay with her, not like that; not with a woman with fish skin all over her body. That's what I said, and I said it calm, like I knew what I was talking about. But I didn't know anything yet. I was just jealous."

I should have felt sorry for Mam, but Ushag had shrunk and her face was blotched and sad and she was there, so I felt sorry for her instead.

"It was cruel because she believed me, being her sister and trained as I was to heal. Then Colm disappeared, and even when they brought his woolen back, she never believed he was dead. I think she thought he'd deserted her. Then I saw her walk into the sea . . . and I thought . . ." My aunt looked at me with eyes like Bo's when I told her to go back home. "Well, you know what I thought."

I just knew my mam would never have drowned herself over a little teasing. "All right," I pointed out. "But she didn't, did she?" I nodded toward the merrow bones. "She still lives."

"But now I don't know which is worse," she wailed at me, giving up all self-control. I felt like reminding her of her own rules about what was worth having feelings over.

"How can you not know whether it's worse for Mam to be dead or alive?" It seemed to me a simple choice.

"If she's dead, she's just dead. If she's alive — she's a live merrow." My aunt rubbed at her face. "With scales. Merrow scales that I treated her for as if she was sick. And tormented her over. Oh, I was so cruel."

She sat down hard with no care for the salt burn or anything else. "And if she lives, she'd want revenge."

"How do you know that?" My aunt's story of her and Ven had such dark twists.

She shrugged. "How could anybody forgive such things?"

I thought for a moment. "Well, Ven Marrey might start by remembering all the good years of plays and games. The trees and wells and servants you played while she was being a princess. She might remember all the healings before Colm came. Anyway," I said, "it doesn't matter now. She's forgiven you, hasn't she?" Truly, she could be dense as thickets.

"How can you know that?" Ushag wiped her nose.

"Well, if you could just open your mind a bit," I told her, rolling my eyes. "She sent Ulf for you, didn't she? She saved him and put him in your gill net."

"Oh," she said, and slowly, slowly her face cleared. Over this one afternoon she'd heard the merrow song and seen the webbed marks in the cave of hands. Now she was face-to-face with the merrow bones. My aunt's rules about what could and couldn't be were crumbling, and finally they just collapsed. Her mind opened. I saw it happen. It was like watching the sun rise in her face. "All right, then. I suppose it must be real," she said, and that was that. I'd proved it.

I'd thought it would feel better than it did.

It was even colder going back through the tunnel than it had been coming, and this time my aunt pushed me through from behind. On the other side, she grabbed the eel bag I'd left behind the day of the earthshake. "Waste not, want not," she said in spite of having just met a merrow, if not in the flesh, then surely in bones. Honor Bright, sometimes I think she just doesn't know what's important.

We ran all the way down the gorge full of some kind of wild humor. The wind had dropped, the sun was setting, and the cove seemed an entirely new place. Back at the house, Ulf was sleeping, but woke to see what we'd bagged up at the pool. Auntie Ushag untied the wriggling bag and tipped our catch onto the floor. It wasn't an eel, after all.

It was a salamander.

CHAPTER FOURTEEN

Trembles

THAT NIGHT MAM CAME TO ME. She knelt by
my bed and put her cool cheek to my hot one.
Her fingertips pushed back the hair sticking to my face
and gently pinched my earlobe to wake me. I heard
her whispering, but the words were lost in fitful winds,
and though I could hear her, I could neither move nor
answer. Then, as in my dream, I heard her calling my
name again. "Daughter," she called, and her voice was
full of laughter. "It's time. Come away." She gave me
a pearl to swallow. It was filled with bubbles. "Wait for
me," she said, and then she was gone. I was alone in
my bed, clammy from the touch of her wet hand.

So I went down into the moonlit cove and waited.
The seal pup came to watch me waiting; an owl, too,
came on silent wings and joined me for a time. I waited
for Mam and the Others all night. I was ready.

A swarm of glowing jellies drifted into the cove. It was a swarm such as had never been seen before on the island. Folk talked of it for years after, but I, who'd been sitting right on the beach where they came closest to land, could never tell a story of them. They were just a wall between Mam and me, and I paced the waterline, troubled that she wouldn't be able to pass through the siege. Were merrows pained by the jellies' stings, or did their scales protect them? I wondered. Over that night, our cove filled with a mile or more of their glowing wash, and then emptied as they flowed out again into the open sea. I was relieved when they were gone. Now Mam could come.

All night I expected her at any moment. The pearl she'd given me bubbled in my belly, ready to feed me air until I grew my gills. Mam would teach me how to sink and rise; my human shape would change, and the deep world would grow me into a sea-dwelling thing. I didn't even mind if it hurt. I would never need the stone sack again.

When Mam came, I'd grow webs between my fingers and toes, and my Scale would spread and cover me. Most likely I'd ride on her back and we'd swim out and float spread-eagled like starfish under the sky together, and we'd talk and we'd sing and the stories would grow in us. We'd dive deeper than otters, deeper than seals, deeper even than whales, and down there we'd play hide-and-seek. I'd be able to fold myself into some gap in the rocks like a crab or spider, but she'd always find me. Down there where the kraken lives, I'd find my real life. It waited for me.

I saw it. Our undersea house made from grit and merrow spit. Mam and me asleep together on a bed of sponges, covered with our rug of featherstars. Us tending the anemone gardens. Her teaching me to sing the high and wild songs. Coming to sing for Auntie Ushag, and leaving her presents from the deepest wrecks. Now that Ulf had come she'd be all right. All right without me.

I waited on.

The sky quickened, but she didn't come.

As the sun broke free of the horizon, the earth gave a groan, and somewhere far away, a rumble started up. Like the lowest voice in the most monstrous throat of the deepest-dwelling rock beast, it rumbled. My heart sank as if it knew something I didn't, and my skin crept on me like it would desert my trembling bones. The shore pitched once, and the sand about me shivered. I heard a low, protesting moan and I looked about for whoever had made the sound, but it had been me. I stood up.

Dust, then rubble, then rocks fell from the cliffs, some into the water and some onto the beach. There

165

was no hiding place. The earth was alive. Down by the water I was safe from falling rock, but the shifting sand meant I had to crawl if I was to move at all. I couldn't take my eyes off the dropping cliff, and so I crawled backward into the sea as Marrey Cove groaned all around me.

Boulders rolled and pinnacles broke; all was grating and thundering. On the northern point, slabs of the cliff slid away and fell right into the sea without a sound, taking vines and gulls and nests with them. Some of the sea caves were blocked by the falling rock, and others were opened. It was becoming a new world. My fear drove me back farther into the water until I had to stop or fall off the drop. I could feel the tow just behind me, and that's when I thought of it.

Perhaps Mam had meant I should wait down there off the drop, safely filled as I was with the breath of the pearl. Perhaps she'd waited all night in the kelp forest for me to prove myself, but I hadn't trusted in her. I'd stayed up in the air, on the shore, and shown I had no faith. I hadn't trusted her, and that's why she hadn't come.

I can't easily tell what happened next. I suppose it seemed to me that she was playing some trick I couldn't win, or giving me some test I couldn't pass, because I turned and shouted at the sea. "Where are you?" The rumbling had passed away, and there was just me and the sound of my voice. I was surprised how loud my voice could be. "It's time," I called. "Mammy . . . it's time." The sea took my words without any sign of hearing them. No arm rose above the waves; no slippery body whipped about me. No lonely voice called back.

She wasn't coming.

It just wasn't fair. I'd fought with Auntie Ushag for her. I'd never believed the stupid market stories about her. I'd stood up for her, and made everybody angry with me. Well, not Ma and Scully, but Ushag and most of Shipton. I wanted to lie down in the sea and pull the waves over me; to close my eyes against the speckled light and know no more of it all. My head hurt, and without a warning, I puked. A strong hand took my arm and another my waist, and I fell into them. My head was swimming.

I felt myself carried back to shore, where I lay drenched and scoured—and empty. The bubbling inside had stopped. Ushag and Ulf leaned over me, their faces full of trouble.

"What were you doing down here?" asked Ushag.

"I was waiting," I told her.

"Waiting? In the middle of an earthshake?" She looked around at the ruined cliffs. "What for?"

"I was waiting for Mam," I said. In spite of my aunt having seen the proof and now being a believer, I was still somewhat windy telling her. However, she didn't fight me. She just sent Ulf for the jug and some dry clothes. And when he'd gone, she took me in her arms and we rocked back and forth for a while. The mother seal had come back into the cove and was watching us, her head bobbing above the water like a dog's and her whiskers drooping. I was too well-grown now to fit in my aunt's lap, or any other part of her, but she managed somehow to hold me, and slowly the sickness settled. She sighed from the heels of her feet up.

"The thing about the Others is they're not like us," she said finally.

"I know that," I muttered, feeling prickly now. "Obviously."

"I don't think you do." She sat by me in the wet sand, and I couldn't help noticing that the face on her was the face of another, altogether softer woman. Something in her had gone; something else had come. I couldn't say what. "You think your mam will come for you. You think she misses you, like you miss her. You think she wants what you want."

She was right, but it didn't stop me from feeling like slapping her. A person's mind should stay their own, and here she was telling me what I had in there.

"What do I want, then, if you're so all-knowing?" I asked her.

"You want to belong," she said quietly, and looked

sideways at me with her black eyes like a gull. For some reason, I felt shamed by that sharp glance. "It's natural to us," she added.

I saw where she was headed. "But not natural to them?"

She was thoughtful. "No, I don't think so. They're wild, see, not trained like dogs . . . or horses . . . or us, for that matter. We think they're something to do with us. We put them in stories . . . but they're our stories, not theirs. They've never even heard them."

I didn't know what to believe. "So the stories are wrong?"

"Well, not wrong, exactly," she said, thinking deeply. "But surely mistaken about the nature of the Others. It seems foolish to blame them for not fitting in with our stories."

Now I was truly all at sea. "But Mam's human. Part human, anyway."

"When the Otherness in a person is forced out into the open, there's no putting it back." She sighed, and I thought, for a person who two days ago was nothing but scornful of "all that earwig," she seemed to know a lot about it now.

"But she's my mother," I said.

She knew what I meant; mothers, human or otherwise, should be there—not cold-bloodedly swanning about in the sea. Mothers should want to be with their children. They should not leave them to grow up all anyhow. I pointed into the cove. "Even the seals know about mothers."

"Well, yes, but she's not a seal, is she? And she's not a mother anymore, Neenie. She's forgotten." Strained now by the long conversation, Auntie Ushag used my child name. "She's not my sister. She's not your mother. She's not a woman; she's not even human. From the moment she went over, we lost her just as surely as if she'd died. They do not live for our benefit. They belong to Themselves."

I remembered the rolling otter and its sweet-looking paws — dashing that urchin with the rock and the blood staining the water. I remembered the jewel-red crab — dragging that scavenged flesh into the sea grass. I'd found them comical, and pretty, but they were their own creatures too, just as my aunt said, and busy with the job of living. They probably didn't even see me. I remembered the way the cave spiders and suchlike scurried to hide from me in the rocks.

They were not there for us. They had their own mysterious life living inside them. Their world was not my world, their story not mine; they had otter thoughts in an otter world, red crab thoughts in a red crab world. Thinking about it made me light-headed.

"I don't know how a person gets to turn fully Otherwise," Auntie Ushag went on. "Perhaps they

have to have the blood to begin with, and then a shock pushes them over. That's how I see it, anyway. That's how it was for Ven. And I don't know how much they remember from before. We could talk of that forever, but the truth is, once a person's gone over, they can't come back . . . they must live the Other life or die."

"But what about the merrow wives?" I asked. "They come in from their Other lives and live a human life. With children," I added. "They live happily ever after. Everybody says."

"Do they?" she asked right back at me, sharp. "Have you truly listened to those stories?"

I didn't know what to say then, and as Ulf returned with the warmed jug, my aunt finished up. "What we do know is that your mam still lives, somewhere in the sea, and that by itself is something to be drinking to, eh?"

I tried to feel happy for it as Ushag plainly did, and I managed a small smile.

"To Ven," she toasted. We each took a swig in turn, and the spice filled my belly with heat. "But, Neen, now it's time."

Suddenly I was cold in spite of the warm mug. It's what Mam had said.

"Time for what?" I asked.

"Time to stop waiting," she told me. "Ven belongs to the Otherworld now." She turned to face the cliff

and looked up toward the yard. "And you belong to this one," she said to the rock and the path. "You belong to the cove—and to me. You belong to your mam's blood, to our blood, but mostly you belong to yourself . . . and to what will come." With that, she started up the sand toward the cliff path and home.

There'd been no pearl; I knew that now. It had all been a dream in a fever at wind-rise. That's what I got for swimming in tunnels of ice water and then spending a whole afternoon dripping wet in cold caves. Ulf put a rug around my shoulders.

"Orraht, Nin? *Góð píka*," he said, his big freckly face all bothered and pink. He really was the sort of person you could get very fond of. I traced the merrow skin picture on the back of his broad hand.

"Sea girl," I muttered to myself.

Ulf wrinkled up his brow like he didn't know what I was saying. I thought he was suffering a Deafness now, on top of everything else.

"Sea girl," I bawled into his ear, and pointed at the skin picture.

"*Nei,*" he said. "*Nei.*" No. He waved his hand toward the water. "Sea girl." Ulf swept the mother seal a deep bow. "Denk yoo, sea girl. Denk yoo." She took absolutely no notice of him.

CHAPTER FIFTEEN

Molting

AUNTIE USHAG HAD A WHOLE NEW FACE on her. She kept giving me the knowing eye, and petting me whenever she passed, and she was talkative too. In fact, she was downright chatty. She went on about the eaves warblers in the roof, the longtails breeding in the stores, and the seals molting in the cove, and cheerfully, too, like these ordinary things were marvels. Flashing from one matter to the next, she would change heading like a school of sprats. She'd never talked about the weather before, but now she seemed tickled pink just to have some.

"I've never known the sun to have such heat in it," she said, which by any measure is a foolish thing to say. What else was it going to have in it? She said things that could be plainly seen by anybody with sense, such as it being a bright morning, or that I was growing. She even sang, and tried to make me sing with her.

Once she danced a jig around the steaming pot on the fire, raising ashes and dust that brought on coughing and more laughing. She was changed. She was happy. I didn't like it.

I kept trying to catch Ulf's eye, but he was too busy watching this new singing, dancing Ushag, and it was plain he didn't know what to make of it. She'd been his prickly nurse, grumbling and growling over the cures; she'd been his grave and silent friend, and now here she was singing and laughing and wearing hats from the wreck trunk to get a laugh. He watched her like sailors watch the sky. And he fetched and carried for her, as I did.

My aunt had set her mind to a feast with the Slevins to mark the finding of the merrow bones. All morning she'd been roasting and steeping, and the house was all steam and smoke. She moved about in it, tasting and spitting, stirring and spicing, like the meat in her own broth. Being a busy sort of person herself and liking it, she naturally tried her best to give us a share of that pleasure too and set us to work. Already I'd scrubbed the steps, Ulf had chopped more wood than we'd use in a month in the heat, and we both had searched the yard and plots, the orchard and even up toward the wood, for the eggs our hens lay wherever they like. Now I'd had enough.

I couldn't stand it anymore. Taking a sack, I said

I'd go gather any useful bits of the seal molt on the shore, and when Ushag said she'd come with me and help, I told her not to. I said she was never going to get all that meat and drink done by sunset anyway, and that set her to proving me wrong. Once she was busy again, I could creep away. I didn't know why I wasn't happy. I should have been.

All summer I'd known the truth about the merrows, hadn't I? And wasn't this what I'd longed for: to be proved right about Mam, for my aunt to believe me and to have the wit to change her mind? Well, now I was right and Ushag did believe, so why wasn't I content? Auntie Ushag's change of mind hadn't changed my humor. In fact, I was even darker in my heart. What was the matter with me?

Everything was changed, but not as I'd expected. Since yesterday's sickness, I'd started to feel that I knew something else that was important, but I couldn't put a pin in it. Whatever it was, it slid around inside my head. Every time I tried to look at it straight, it would change shape or slip away. If I could just calm myself, I could winkle it out; I could know what this new thing was.

Along with Ushag, Marrey Cove was changed too. It had a new face of caves and rubble. Black sand from the top of the cliff was now dirtying the sand at its base, and it was different in other ways too. There'd been some sort of monstrous tide in the night, in spite of it being the wrong moon for such things. The high-water mark was right up at the cliff itself, marked by a wall of thick and tangled weed. I had to climb over it to get down to the sea, and the stench was like Shipton harbor at the end of a summer market.

It looked like a slaughter on the sand, with some creatures gaping their jaws and flapping now and then and others not moving at all. There were all the common fish and crabs but in uncommon numbers: pollack, dogfish, tope, and conger wrecked on the sand and already greening in the sun. There were creatures I'd never seen, such as a tiny thing like a shrunken kraken whose eyes were half its body, and a sort of fish like a lump of wood and with a bucket mouth as big as its whole head and full of needle teeth. There was one of these with a smaller one of its kind stuck to its side through some type of pipe. There were giant turtles, and washed up at the end of the cove, right at the waterline, there was a whale.

It was a terrible thing to see them all stranded like that. I felt as I did when Auntie Ushag skinned rabbits, pulling them wholly out of their hides in one go and throwing their small, bare bodies into a basin at her feet. I always wanted to slip their coats back on and see them scut away back to the hills and hollows, living again. Soft feelings butter no parsnips, my aunt would say in those days, watching me battle between my sympathy and my hunger. Of course, then the stew would come and those feelings would fade with good smells and a grumbling belly. I didn't know what she would say now, before such waste.

I moved around the broken cove, gathering bits of the molt. Much of the hide had been torn in last night's violent tide, but there were still some strips that would be useful enough. Following the waterline, I found the mother seal sheltering in a nest of rock in the cliff's shadow. Her fur was hanging from her in festoons, and the hind skin was sore and angry-looking. I didn't see her pup. She didn't move away, only lay gazing at me with big, black eyes as I fetched from by her side a sizable piece of her own speckled hide.

That seal was so lazy and unafraid there, and I felt like I'd never rest again. At that moment, her peaceful harbor seemed to me the most desirable thing in the world. To have somewhere safe and right to call home, to be a seal among seals, and to be undisturbed by the presence of those who are otherwise; it seemed an impossible thing. I was sick of being this split thing, a human tormented by all the stories of her kind. I lay down in the cool sand near the seal and listened to her breathing.

Behind us, the caves opened into the cliff. An onshore breeze picked up and gently blew the molt and flotsam around. I heard a whistling among the rocky halls, and then a hollow hum, and as I listened, it grew into a low song. The caves were singing. I lay there listening and patting my hands into the still-damp sand. I squeezed handfuls of the sand and, when I opened them, saw the shape and lines of my own fist marked there. It calmed me, and I thought perhaps now I could pin that slippery new thought of mine.

I sat up and felt the breeze strengthen. All around me were my hand marks in the damp sand. As the cave song waxed and waned, I was caught in the lazy humor of the seal. I traced around my own hand marks, and then idly I added to them. I turned them into anemone gardens and tiny kraken. I turned them into stars and starfish. I turned them into families of five, all with a thumb mother. I drew webs between some fingers, and claws at the tips of others. Close by, the seal snorted and rolled onto her side to watch me.

Then, behind the wall of weed, I saw an odd fish.

I'd thought it was another rock, with its rough shape and lumpy skin. Its head was huge and flat like a grindstone, and it had tiny legs and arms just as if it were natural for some fish to do so. Its tail had been torn off somewhere, but the rest was so big and fresh, I couldn't leave it there for the gulls. The broth we made from it would feed us for a week. I crammed it into the sack with the molt.

The breeze that had picked up now dropped away, as is always the way these days. Sometimes I'd give anything just to feel a good wet wind and a fall of cold rain. I vowed to welcome the winter hag this year without one whine about ice or gales. Ushag would have a new wet-cloak made from the seal's cast-offs, but I planned to go blue-toed and goose-pimpled right up until Christmas. It's strange how in the middle of a hot spell you can forget what it feels like to be cold.

As I hefted the stinking sack back through the mazy rocks, I passed where I'd been sitting. My hand marks stood out in the clear lines and shadows of summery midday. I couldn't help noticing that the webbed ones were just like those in the cave of hands. In a moment, the slippery thought that had been tormenting me stopped long enough to grasp—and my calm was gone.

What if?

What if the wind in the cliffs could have sung the merrow song? What if the webbed hands could have been drawn there by some Old one drawing a story, or just doodling like I had been? I raised my eyes to meet those of the mother seal. She nosed at the air and barked. Without warning, her pup, now almost fully grown, appeared at my side. He pushed past me on his way to her, and both creatures made sounds of welcome. I felt the old pain on the matter of mothers and children, but this time I was dry-eyed. There were more important things to think about.

What if the merrow bones weren't?

In some tricky reversal, whereas before I had been filled right up with knowledge, now I was brimful with doubt. That slippery thought had upturned everything. I had believed there were no other explanations for all I'd found, but with a doom-filled upside-down feeling, now I saw nothing but other explanations for everything. Like all those rotting sea things in the wall of weed, my proof was falling apart.

On the way back, I was plagued by Auntie Ushag's shining, we-share-a-secret face and her glad eyes, haunted by her petting and singing and laughter. I tipped that odd fish back into the piles of weed. I didn't know what I knew anymore, and that was a fact.

CHAPTER SIXTEEN

Undertow

THE SUN WAS NOW STRAIGHT overhead. If I didn't know better, I'd have sworn the world and it were drawing closer. Like the full moon, it almost filled one half of the sky and blazed so that I couldn't even look at it sideways. I just felt it hanging there behind me, dripping heat like candle wax down my neck as I walked. It had no pity, and under its rays all the dead of last night's great tide had shriveled to black guts and silvery-fine fish leather. The stink off them seemed to walk abroad like it was its own creature, with weight and a will of its own. It followed me along the shore, poking me in the nose and mouth, tickling my throat with its stenchy fingers until I had to cover my face.

Honor Bright, I never smelled anything like it, not even that time I found the fallen cow up the gorge.

The Prior's hell with all its brimstone and corruption would have to work hard to match it.

Near the water, the stink thinned out somewhat and I could breathe again without gagging. Today the sea was blue, and out in the cove, the whitecaps tossed out ribbons of lacy spray. Farther still, and ripples broke against hidden rock and tiny reef, but up close to the shore, all was flat as a board and clear. I could see down to the white sand bed, its stones and shells, and all the darting schools sheltering there. I stood still in the shallows and let the tiny fish nibble my toes. If you let them, they will have all the dead and hanging skin right off you. To them, it's dinner.

I was alone. Every other living thing on the beach was hiding from the sun. Crowding gulls and all the rock-pool creatures seemed to have been taken from the world overnight, and all I could hear were ripples and, far, far away, a hum of insects. My head was surging and the path home suddenly seemed too long and too rough, the cliff, too steep and rocky, and I saw only obstacles and breathless heat that way. Giving up, I dropped the molt sack on the rocks and waded into the big, cool sea.

It was a strange thing to stand in water exactly the color of the sky, strange not to be able to see a horizon. The unending blue stretching before, above, and to each side of me made me light-headed. Without edges, the middle disappears. I felt myself floating there inside the blue, everywhere and nowhere at one time. It made me dizzy, so I looked down at my feet. My brown toes spread like fingers into the earth and gripped like roots. The sand was still solid, if shifting, and the nibbling fish at least were real.

I splashed pleasurably forward, sighing aloud as each water drop hit my skin, and the fact is I was so taken with the coolness, I forgot to look where I was going. In spite of being a noticing sort of person, I didn't see the ground fall right away just before me. Not only had the shoreline and cliffs changed their face in the earthshake, but now the undersea parts were changing too. I hadn't taken ten pleasant, cooling steps with eyes half-closed before I fell off the new drop edge.

Before this day, the drop had been a fair way out and could always be trusted to be where it was last time. A line of waving kelp marked a spot ten paces beyond where the ground fell away, and you could walk safe up to its very edge. The drop moves about now, and on that day, it had moved closer to the shore. Without warning, I stepped into nothing. As I sank, I glimpsed only the mess of weed and the pit of dark water beneath me.

I wasn't scared at first, just surprised. Straightaway I kicked up into the light and toward what I thought would be the shore, but when I breached, I wasn't anywhere near the cliff path. I didn't know where I was. The molt sack had gone. I couldn't see the shattered beach at all. I was in a storm of water, wrack, and grit, rolling toward the far cliff and out into broad water, traveling fast. The new drop had delivered me right into the undertow.

The world and all its parts slowed. I struggled against the tow's terrible drag, but every thrash and strike just sucked strength from me while doing nothing to move me one span closer to still waters. Every time I was spat to the surface, I sucked in air like a gale before being pulled back into a slow boil of foam and strangling weed. I was rolling and flipping, wrapped and unwrapped in flotsam, but slow, slow, like in dreams. The kelp streamed by, graceful as water snakes, the foam forming itself into shapes in the water just as clouds do in the sky. I even had the time to admire them. My own hair wrapped itself around my face, blinding me, or wriggled and twisted upward around my head like a meadow of glass eels.

At last the tow pushed me to the seabed and pinned me there. Spread-eagled under countless weights of water, flayed by the shell grit, then scoured by stinging salt, I felt myself finally run out of puff. I was done in. It was over. I stopped fighting.

It was a relief to do so. As I watched with interest the water above me dapple and dim, I wondered what was to happen next. I had always thought of death as something that happened to old people, or the sick, or those whose job it was to kill and die, such as raiders or soldiers. Stories, of course, were filled with folk dying, but that was just part of the fun. It was something that happened to other people. Now here I was, dying. There was nothing to be done, and so I did that. The world flowed away from me, there was a rushing, and then I noticed and wondered no more.

I was dragged along a tunnel toward a soft light, where somebody was waiting for me, and I expected to find myself in a glowing crystal cave or some such holy place filled with sweet smells and harmonious chanters—but I was spat out in a cow byre. They say paradise and earth are only three feet apart, and now I saw what they meant. What I supposed to be my own paradise was very like home: darkish and sizable, and smelling strongly of dung, straw, and warm cow. And why wouldn't it, because at the far end was the biggest cow I'd ever seen. Her head was twice the size of other cows, even the breeds up the Cronks, and I guessed she stood over me by one whole grown man. Her hooves were as foundation stones, and her udders as a giant's bagpipes. She was plainly filled with milk and lowing irritably, so I grabbed the stool and bucket and started milking her. It seemed like a good idea, in spite of being dead.

That mountainous cow filled the bucket easily and then was done with me, turning her back and chewing her cud as though I weren't there. A door behind her swung open, and stone steps circled downward into the earth. I didn't have to think about what to do— a door opened and I went in, a cow turned up and I milked it, and now these stone steps fronted me. There was nothing to do but follow them, so I did. I carried the bucket without spilling a drop until I reached the very bottom. And there, in the soft light of a forest of slender and glowing mushrooms, waited for me a shrunken and ancient woman.

She reached only to my elbow, but when she came closer, I saw that she was bent sharply from the hips and that was the reason for her lack of height. With her eyes brown as new-tilled earth, and fat as a goose like she'd never known hunger, she had the air of content all over her. Her skin was as warm wood, ringed and scored with great age, and her chest was bigger than the baker's Cushie; although plainly not under the rule of the world anymore, I was still a bit disgusted when she reached out with both arms and clutched me into it. The Ancient one held me there and laughed like bells, not tinkling bells but ships' bells or church bells. She pealed and tolled, loud and important. "Give me my due, Mortal Child," she clanged. "And we'll see what's to be done with you."

Seeing me casting about for what she could possibly mean, the little woman waved her hand toward the far wall. There, almost hidden by drooping fern, was the stone bowl from Ma's altar. It was empty and carved in spirals and knots. I knew what I needed to do now. Lifting the bucket, I poured the giant cow's milk into the stone bowl.

At once, the room below the byre flooded with light. Breeshey, for that was who it was, came to the bowl and smiled up at me. Taking a stone mug, hollowed out with great skill and worn on one side from an endless progress of mouths, she scooped and drank deeply from the still-warm milk. Then she gave me the mug, and I did the same. The Ancient one dipped her fingers into the bowl then and marked my brow with the same spiral as the stone bowl. The quiet room, the old woman, the warm milk; they all lulled me into a kind of senselessness. Then, out of nowhere, she took up a bright and curved blade.

My senses returned in a moment. "No!" I started back from her, but Breeshey grabbed my hand and held it over the stone bowl. She drew the blade over my palm, and with a sharp pain, the blood came.

"Yes. Yes, yes . . ." She hummed and stroked my

cheek as the blood dropped into the milk and stained it with red ribbons. "There. It's done." She poked me in the ribs, hard, and the room filled with her laughter. It was a charm, and I couldn't help myself; I had to laugh too. It all suddenly struck me as deeply comical, though I couldn't have said what or why. She thumped me on the back, once, twice, and then, with one last backbone-breaking thump, I was bursting, laughing face-first into the light and spray of Marrey Cove.

I wasn't dead anymore. I was alive—but still dragging away in the undertow. There were dead fish raging all around me, and I felt like something in one of Ma's stews. And I was still being thumped upward from underneath. I tried grabbing at whatever was thumping me, but whenever I gripped at it, my hands just slid off.

Each of these thumps nearly broke a rib, and I set my mind to thumping it back the very next time it rose. Instead, as it rose under my belly, I gripped around its broad neck, thinking to stop it diving again, and I just held on like a limpet. The slippery creature dipped its head, flipped its tail, and was away. I got my arms around its neck and clung on with little hope, every instant expecting to be stolen away into the wide sea. We moved through the water storm like the lightest and sleekest of the raiders' ships. I rode on its back, casting wakes on each side and my nose stinging from salt and wind. Straight and true we cut through the undertow, and then I was dumped, gasping for breath, choking, puking, into the clear shallows of the little inlet. When I could, I looked to see what it was that had carried me from my death back to my life.

The mother seal rolled in the shallows only a few steps away, nodding and blinking in the light. She heaved herself over to me, and for one moment she gave me the eye, face-to-face. Her gaze was sharp, part amused and part troubled. It was the same eye I'd seen her give her pup. It was the same eye Ushag gave me when listening to me talk story. Not this summer's stories — they had proved to be mostly troubling, and not very comical — but the stories before this summer, the stories of my childhood. The mother seal rolled onto her back and barked. From the mazy rocks came her pup, out of nowhere.

"Thank you, sea girl," I said as she turned her speckled back to me and greeted him. Then they were away through the weed and swelling water. I watched their bubble trails move into the cove, and then I turned to see how I was placed.

My heart had been cherishing that little inlet. I was the only one who had truly seen its perfection, and for a long time I had longed to claim its white and silver perfection for myself. But now I was here and it was just another beach, and even messier and dirtier than

Marrey Cove. Its dangling vines had dried out and hung to the cliff walls like smoked eels in a lean-to. Its white sands, pocked by rubble, were now grey. The tidal dead blotted the sand. My dream of the little inlet was finished. Now I just wanted to go home.

Just out past the rocks, the undertow thundered on, all foam and spit. I would not get home that way. I turned to the cliff face.

It was as if some child giant had taken its hammer and battered at the rock in a temper. It was more holes than cliff now. Rocks the size of houses had fallen to its base, and the mountain's insides were plain to see. Winding tunnels burrowed through its body, like the trails left by wood ants in bodge, and hived into count- less tiny cells, like a lump of honeycomb. Just above my head, a gap as tall as oaks had been shaken out of the rock, and beyond that, a cave opened up into ledged walls and a soaring roof. It looked big enough to hold all sorts of things, perhaps even a way out.

First, though, I had to clamber up and over all the fallen rock. It was overhot, as I think I've mentioned before, and I was trembling all over from my rough swim, not to mention the events of Breeshey's byre. There was no mother seal to help me here, and no Ushag. I was going to have to save myself.

Some of those boulders were smooth as eggshells, and I had to search for the tiniest of toeholds and grips to climb them; others were sharp as flints, and if I was to go on, I just had to let myself be cut. There was nothing else to do. My sweating body slipped often, but I found that if I breathed very slowly and didn't think of anything beyond this grip, this toehold, I could do it. Pulling myself up over the last rim of the last rock, I lay still for some time, waiting for my heart to settle. I'd been scared of being stuck in the inlet until Ushag noticed I was gone, a thing she might not have done for a whole day and night or more, in that we don't live in each other's shadows. I stood and limped over to the opening, where my heart leaped like a hare and I couldn't hold back from laughing. I knew this cave.

It was the cave of the merrow bones; well, that is, it was and it wasn't. The gap did lead into the cave but somewhat up the height of its walls, and so I was looking down into it from a deep shelf. It was the same cave in spite of the changes wrought by the earth-shakes; I could see the dark pool at its far end, and the pit of dead things with its flies. I sat on the edge of a rock shelf and let myself drop into the sand. Straightaway the burning started, and I ran on my toes to the pool, where I rested and watered my feet.

There'd been a big fall of rock, and the pit of shoes was gone under rubble. I couldn't see any sign of the merrow bones. It was now just an ordinary cave.

I was going to have to swim the tunnel by myself and hope that I hadn't grown much in the last few days. There hadn't been much room last time, and my aunt was fond of pointing out that lately I grew more like a heifer than a human. The water of the dark pool was still, cold, and sour, and I gazed into it, waiting for my belly to catch up with my head. My head was sure and set in my course; my belly was all *but* and *what if*.

My own face stared back at me from the pool, and I wondered for the first time whether I was well-grown or not. I couldn't tell. The words of the market women troubled me. Not that I cared, but I didn't think I looked anything like a wood violet. I'm small and dark like Ushag and Ven—and violets, come to think of it—but I think I look more like a fox or a longtail. I don't know why those women in Shipton have to turn everything into a romance. Ushag said the only thing a body might need to look like a wood violet for is getting a certain type of man, and for everything else it just gets in the way. She said women don't like other women who look like wood violets, and that decent men look for more than indecent measures of floweriness in their women. She said it takes so long to cultivate the violet in a body that there's no time to fill the pot or see to the yard.

She also said I should look at a wood violet's life before I got myself set on becoming one. I did; they live in the dark their entire lives and aren't good for much apart from adornment. I closed my eyes and splashed my face. After all the salt, even that sour water felt good.

When I opened them, there was a new, white face staring up at me. Its lips were pulled into a snarl; I could see all its teeth. I scrabbled backward, away from the pool and it, and hid behind a rock to see what the white face was going to do. I watched, but nothing came up out of the water, and after some time waiting, I crept back to the pool and looked over its edge. The face was still there, but it hadn't moved. I started to think it must be dead, and stirred the water a bit with my hand, and then I saw the truth. It was not in the water but was reflected in it from behind and above me.

Now I spun on my heels with my breath turning to ice in my throat. The beastly face was staring at me from the shelf above. Its eyes were hollow. I felt around for some weapon and put my hand to a rock.

Letting out a savage scream, which shook the rubble further and showered me with dust, I hurled that rock like my aunt hurls the gill net. It went straight and true and hit that face full in its nose. There was a hollow clatter, and the face, along with the whole head belonging to it, fell into the pool. I had knocked the thing off entirely. Now I was filled with a different sort of horror and scrambled backward out of the pool, away from the head. It bobbed in the water, with its black eyes staring. Then I stopped. Its eyes were not just black and empty but really hollow; that is, it had no eyeballs.

It was a head, but it wasn't alive. It wasn't even a proper head. It was just a skull; a human skull.

CHAPTER SEVENTEEN

Bones

I DID THINK ABOUT GETTING OUT of there right then, before that skull could do something like talk. I didn't want to hear anything it had to say, even if its head was now brimful with wisdom and help for such as me. Before any of Ma's walking dead could prove themselves to me, or the Others came swarming like jellies, I wanted to be out in the common world under a regular sun.

I didn't want to meet any of the drowned crofters who walked the undersea paths. I didn't want to see their sad, swinging lanterns, nor have any of them choose me as a companion. I wanted no brokenhearted cave-dwelling ancestors to find and hold me there to warm their cold, cloven hearts. I didn't want to hear the banshee Scully told me about. Suddenly I didn't feel proud to be a Marrey, stuck in our cove of bafflement. I just wanted to get out.

I could have wriggled through the tunnel and been away down the gorge, safely back in our yard before another stone could drop in Carrick, before another great tide could wash in or another hot cloud of dust settle. I was stuffed to the gullet with the gods, water spirits and cave ghosts, seafolk, faery, and all their kind. I just wanted something to be real. With my fear turning to anger, I fished the skull from the dark pool.

Where there was a head, there was bound to be a body. There was no running away from that fact. My reckless legs were scrambling up the rubble before my craven belly could stop them. As I did, shocks of clattering stone ran around the cavern and sounded through all its chimneys and chambers.

The skull had brought with it an Otherwise humor. Anything could live in that beehive underworld for a lifetime and never be found. I half expected tribes of bloodless cave folk, dwarfish men and pale, hovering women, to swarm over me like ants and carry me off to tend their slug-like offspring. Or a giant spider to take me delicately between his feet and wrap me in white web and hang me like our rabbits in his larder. Or at the very least, a blood-hungry landlocked eel to rise from the pool and eat every part of me. But there was nothing, just the sound of dripping damp and my own sliding footfalls, and sometimes the dark pool bubbling a little. As I cleared the rock slip, though, all the ghouls of my mind's eye melted away.

The fact is, on the rock shelf above the dark pool was spread before me a skeleton, an entire set of somebody's bones. I tried to look upon it lightly, as though the burden of my eyes might wake it up. It was all there down to the smallest toe bone, and lying about it, as if likewise dead, were the rags that were once its clothing. There was even, here and there, a tiny rag of its skin still clinging to a rib or a knee.

I've seen lots of dead things, but it still gives me a sad surprise to see how small a creature looks when all that's left is its bones. The life in a body is so much more than blood and bone; you can only see that plain and clear when life has gone. In spite of Ma and the Prior being so certain about where folk go when they die (the Prior says he's going to Christ's heaven, and Ma's all for going west, while Auntie Ushag says she's got enough to do here and now and she hopes whatever happens next, she gets to rest), I've always found it a bit of a mystery where all the life goes. Everything seems made of the same stuff when it's dead: rabbits, fish, insects — people. The rabbit-ness is gone, the fish-ness is gone and all that made it whatever it was, and all that's left is this thing like a rock or a stick. Boneclad, everything becomes unified somehow.

This human was no different. It was small. It was dry. It was like part of the rock.

How did the bones end up on this rock shelf in the middle of a mountain? Did it walk in and somehow get knocked senseless and die? But why would it have climbed up onto the rock shelf first? Perhaps it swam through the tunnel—but then what? I supposed it could have been carried in from outside and dumped on the shelf, perhaps by wreckers or raiders. It didn't seem likely. Ushag would have remembered strangers in the cove; though she may have set herself not to tell me if she didn't want me fearful. It may have been a high tide or a giant wave, but it would've had to fill this cave and rise right over the rock shelf for a body to sink and then settle onto it. The tide would have had to ebb slowly so as not to drag the body back to the sea.

It had made peaceful bones, though. It looked like it had been there for years, impossible to say how many. The bones were dried out and scored in wriggle-work. They had fallen to bits: the backbones dropping from their string one by one, the shoulders and ribs collapsing into the grit along with knee bones, hips, ankles, and even the toe bones lying singular and orderly by the feet where they'd fallen. From where I stood, along the shelf a little, it looked like a drawing of a skeleton in the sand. I could see the dent where the head had rested. Something gleamed there in that shadow, and I crawled closer to see, with the skull under my arm.

Before I reached halfway, I knew.

A yell got stuck in my gullet, and I couldn't breathe. Like something out of Ushag's traps, I was both skinned and gutted. Held in the thinnest of sacks and bound together by the finest of wires, slowly my own bones filled with doom and revolt.

A pair of silver hoops lay in the sand. They were silver hoops such as some women down south wear in their ears, but finer wrought and very beautiful. Ear hoops such as these were for special days. I gagged, just once.

I leaned against the rock wall. Ice and heat moved up and down me; parts of me froze or burned in turn. Making some strangled, drawn-out sound, I crawled on until I reached her. I put her skull back with her body. Her skull lay with the rest of her but now rested on its cheek, staring blankly into the cave. I straightened it so that it lay staring upward once more, like somebody decently dead and laid out at a wake. I picked up the ear hoops, cold and hard, not like a stone but like thin ice on the lake. Good silver. Worth something.

Colm had bought them for her with half a season's earnings. She was dead; she was dead. A great quiet consumed me.

I heard every drip down the cold walls, every whistle of wind through the gap, and far off I heard the sea hissing up the beach, but to me there was only one real thing in the world. Mam was dead. Here she was. There was no quarreling with bones.

I picked up one of her finger bones. It was so small, like a child's, and I waited for the tears to fall, or the wailing to start, but nothing happened. I felt I should have been feeling something—even Auntie Ushag would think it worth having feelings over this. But I just felt empty. There was only a whisper in the back of my mind that told me I'd always known.

My hands picked up the skull again, and for an instant, I did want to smash it to bits—but it was just a skull. There was nothing of the woman, the sister, the mother left in it. It was all one with every other dead thing.

Poor Ven. I didn't know her at all. Once, these bones had been covered with her skin and flesh; in other days, I had been borne within those hips. Her eyes had watched me from within their bony hollows. Those tiny hand bones had swaddled me. I brought the skull to my own face until we were nose bone to nose bone and eye hollow to eye hollow. This skull had sat upon that neck and rattled with fancies rather than stones. Where were the stories now? Where were all the plays and games? Had she really walked Carrick on those dried-out grey bones: down south, up the moaney, through the Cronks, around the cove, and at the last, had they really walked her into the sea? Could they have walked her in here, and tucked her away on this rock shelf to die of a broken heart? The fact is, I couldn't remember anything real about her. Not even the face that would have hung on these bones. I had only the stories. A tear fell.

I cried three tears for Mam, and then I remembered Ushag, and the tears dried up. What was I going to tell her? Mam's bones proved her human after all.

The living turn quickly from the dead. We can sit deathwatch for a time, but at last their great absence will remind us that we are still present, and we will need to get on with being so. Life is not fussy about where it grows, but it is set hard on doing so. Stuck now in a tidal cave in a tow-bound inlet with only Mam's bones for company and the sky darkening outside, it dawned on me that I was alive. That is, of course I'd known it like you know that sort of thing, without really thinking about it, but now, in the wake of the undertow and faced with the bones, I felt it pulsing through me: *Live,* it said. *Live.*

I was, in an instant, all common sense and something like courage.

There was only one way out. I had to swim that tunnel by myself, or stay and likely turn to bones myself before they found me. There was no point in being fearful; I would either make it or not, and dwelling on it would make no difference. Soft feelings butter no parsnips. I was cold, I was hungry, and I wanted to be out of my rough tomb and under the broad sky again. Giving myself no time to think more about it, I put my mother's skull back with the rest of her and scrabbled down the fallen rock into the dark pool.

Once more, the deep aches and icy trembles shook my body. Strangely, I didn't care as much as last time, and this is why: I knew then that only the living get to feel aches and trembles. I took the biggest lungful I could and sank again into the black water. The tunnel seemed to reach out to me, and I pulled myself into it with all my will and strength. Straightaway I got stuck.

My shoulders were as a bung, almost stopping the water flowing through the tunnel, and I could go neither forward nor backward. I pushed hard with my feet and pulled with my fists, but I just scraped away my shoulders and hips on the tunnel walls. Every moment, I expected another salamander to snake out of some tight, dark place and curse me with its fevers, face-to-face, where I couldn't turn around. My body had become like the rock itself with the fear. Using all my strength, I still couldn't move. I would need to find another way, and quickly.

Out of my memory rose all those creatures I'd seen wriggle and fold into tiny places: spiders, crabs, eels, and suchlike. I closed my eyes, let my body soften as it had under the weight of the undertow, and tried a snaky wriggle of my legs and hips. My body slid forward half a span. The jelly goddess softened me, the eel goddess lent me her slipperiness, and the spider god gave each of my fingers the gift of creeping and suckering. Struggling against ice and fear and breathlessness, I prayed and snaked my way through the tunnel. My body became as waves rolling from my head to my feet, and I shot forward upon them, my shoulders freed and my lungs bursting. The rest was simple. I spluttered up into the dark of the cave of hands.

The dark outside the cave was almost complete. I would have to goat-foot it down the gorge. My feet carried me through a twilit world of carved spirals and slippery green river stone. I stepped high and sure like Scully right through that dim place. There was no stopping to doubt even one footfall; if I'd stopped, I'd not have known how to start up again, and I believe I'd have just stayed there. In and out of Ushag's shortcut, past the trees reaching to the light, past the vines drooping to the water, in and out of the stream until the light went entirely, and even then I just kept walking. I'd played at being Scully enough to know he never stopped. He kept walking, no matter what, and that was the secret to getting somewhere.

Warmth held in the rocks guided me, and echoes bouncing from each wall kept me straight. At its bottom, the gorge opened out, and I could make out the sea ruffling under a bright young moon-wake. The horizon groaned under sky towers of storm cloud, and though for the moment Carrick's skies were clear, I stood in the stream and hoped with all my heart for real storms and rain. Down by the waterline, someone laughed freely and far-carrying. Lightning lit the cove like full day, and in that blaze I saw Ushag and Ulf. They were dots on the shore, playing in the place between the silver sea and black sky.

She was running toward the sea, with Ulf close behind. She could easily have escaped him, wounded and slow as he was, but I plainly saw her slow her steps on purpose. When he reached her, she darted behind him, making him turn and spin. Then, unlikely as it seems, she leaped like a hare onto his back and buried her hands in his hair. Galloping up and down the sand, he was like a big yellow-maned horse and my aunt his small dark rider. Into the foaming breakers he dashed with her clinging to him. In a moment, they had company.

The mother seal and her pup were circling them. Rising in shining drops and then slapping the water with their falling bodies, they buffeted Ulf and Ushag, who clung to each other at the center of the whirlpool, still laughing. I couldn't tell if the seals were playing or besieging them, and I ran the last steps down to the waterline, but I needn't have been troubled.

The seals were farewelling each other, and the people had gotten in the way.

The pup was now as big as his mother, and it was time for them to leave each other and the cove. Their circling closed until they brushed against each other, and the water foamed where they played and touched for the last time. The pup was the first to go, diving away from his mother like he was throwing himself. His body formed a curve hanging in the air, sheets of water ran from his flanks, and then he dropped and was away in a stream of bubbles. His mother rolled on her back, watching him, and called as long as he was in the cove.

Then she turned to us with her black eyes glimmering and her fluke waving. Her speckled body heaved and sank; her eyes were the last of her left above the water. Then the lightning cracked, the sea was as quicksilver, and she was gone. There were no bubbles to mark her trail.

All summer I'd threshed through the older ones'

stories, picking out the grains of truth in their murders, merrows, kraken, and water horses, their suicides, undersea paths, and Otherworlds. It had boiled away inside me just as if it were natural for a body to hold such a mess. I was almost used to it; it was like I'd learned to live in many worlds at once. I was often somewhat baffled, but also tranced, by it all.

Auntie Ushag, though—she likes everything to be singular and whole. She likes one story for each thing, with a good fit and nothing left over. She'd had her story about Ven all sorted out; it may have grown her into a misery, but at least it was her story, and she knew where she was with it. Then along I came.

Poor Ushag. She had been right all along. Now she was wrong, but how could I tell her?

The shock of finding that Ven still lived would be nothing to the shock of finding her sister to be dead again. She'd smiled more in the one day since we'd found the merrow bones than over the last ten years. I saw her singing cheerfully over the pot at home, cheeking and fussing at Ulf, and petting me. I saw her remembering Ven and smiling to herself. Now she was out dancing on the sand and playing in the sea. If I told her the truth, would she throw Ulf out? Would she clamp her mouth and never talk again? Would she ever forgive me? Perhaps she would send me away.

Perhaps she would just get up and walk away herself. Perhaps she would follow her sister. It was all my fault. What was I to do? Poor Auntie.

Would she want to be wrong and happy, or right and miserable?

CHAPTER EIGHTEEN

Breakers

ULF HAD BUILT THE FEAST FIRE in a clearing among the hazels, and he stood now in its blaze watching it light a circle of trunks and limbs and faces. The faces belonged to Scully and Ma, who sat wrapped in a rug against an alder, her pipe smoke curling upward in the firelight, and the Prior. My aunt had dragged all the embroidered curtains and thick tapestries from the wreck trunk. The rambling roses and leaping hares of the curtains hung between the trees and waved and flapped with the puffs of warm sea air off the cove. The white stags, wolfhounds, and hunting parties of the tapestries covered the ground with their stories. Ulf's bonfire smelled of applewood, and once inside the grove, we were encompassed entirely by Ushag's feast.

I had never seen such a spread. There was a spit stretching across the deepest embers, and along it, rabbits roasted, dripping fat and filling my mouth with water. There was one each. Smallish clay balls baked in the embers. Soon we would open them and, with a lot of smacking of lips and pulling away of prickles, devour the hedge pig inside. There was already a dish of collops, from which everybody picked bare-fingered and greasy, and the roots were buttered and salted in their pot on the ground, next to what smelled to be a sea broth rich in herbs and even adorned with wood violets. I'd never known my aunt to adorn food before.

There was even a hare in a jug, all hacked up and seethed in mead and spices from Shipton market, and a salad of burnet, brooklime, and suckery. My aunt doesn't commonly use such things, saying that raw food is unhealthy and unnatural, but she had made an exception because of the uncommon weather. She thought it would do us good to eat something cool in the heat. Suddenly I was hungrier than I had been for weeks, and I sat, laying Mam's finger bone by me in the grass, filled my trencher, and tucked in.

I would think what to do about Mam's bones later. Everybody was happy and stuffing themselves right now. I couldn't spoil it. We ate in silence, with only the sound of the fire, our chewing and spitting, and the wind rising in the hazels. Halfway through the jug hare, Ushag lifted her mug and spoke.

"I'm glad you've come, and you're welcome to my house. Every one of you." She gave us a gracious face, and we nodded and drank, our mouths larded with weed and eel flesh, as we all toasted the feast. We waited. She'd started talking in the Old way, and now we expected her to keep on. She did her best, in spite of a red face and a mouthful of stutters. "What is mine is yours, as it was in better days, and I hope you won't be leaving before you've eaten all of this and grown new bellies to keep it in."

Our laugh seemed to ease her.

"Anyway, you know how all that rigmarole goes. And while you're eating, I have a story for you." We all stopped eating, and Ma and I swapped troubled glances.

"I know," said Ushag. "But you'll like this one. It's new. It's never been told before."

"We're listening," I mumbled through mouthfuls of rabbit.

"All right," she said. "Here goes.

"I have a friend who, in the course of her youth, misplaced all her happy memories. They were quite lost to her through accidents in her childhood, this woman, and she'd lived without them her whole life and never thought to miss them. In recent days, she made a remarkable journey together with a young kinswoman: a daughter of their house, and the one who would inherit the holding and everything in it."

"Oh, a journey story," whispered Ma to me.

"Any mother, mortal or fish or otherwise, would have been proud to claim this girl. This woman I know was proud, but part of that pride was because she herself had once been just like this young one. She felt that she herself had something to do with the girl's delightful qualities. The girl was tall and strong; she could hurl the net and tend the byre; she could chop wood and build the fire; she could butcher and store meat, and work wood and sharpen blades. She had good wits and liked to sit and think about why and how and so forth. The girl was bighearted; she knew the ways of the bees and talked with birds and seals; the poor knew her to be their friend and the weak were drawn to her; she saw the liars and the cruel ones for what they were. Her face was brown like the Old ones', her hair hung black like shading vines on each side of her face, and her eyes were dark and true of gaze. The woman looked at her and felt content for the future."

I drooped my face to my food. I could feel everybody looking at me.

"But the girl wanted the woman, my friend, to have her happy memories back so they could remember them together at their hearth. She knew their story, the story she would one day tell her children, couldn't be complete without these memories, so she asked the woman to go with her to search them out.

"The journey took a long road right through a country where folks talk in riddles, the whole country thinking it uncivil to speak plain and direct. They passed by an abbey where all the monks walk a foot above the earth and take their own crown of cloud with them, like the tallest of the Cronks. They keep a stable full of high, white horses with bloodred mouths, all of them as swift as swallows, which they ride only to Sunday chapel. They were even carried part of the way by a north wind that sang in human tones.

"There was nothing on the earth to remind the woman, my friend, where or what her memories might be.

"So finally they came to journey inside the earth, where they were witness to many other wonders, among them a dark palace full of invisible beings who could shrink themselves into holes and take Other forms. These Invisibles had once lived in the Bright Halls but had been exiled, and sentenced to fade. Now all that remained of their brightness were the silver hand marks on the dark walls, left from trying to feel their way. The woman and the girl met with dangers there and Other troubles. For instance, they were once tricked by a salamander."

"I told you so," said Ma, sucking the last of the hare off its bones and relighting her pipe. "I'm not gloating, mind you," she added gloatingly. "Never, never trust a salamander." She rocked a little and muttered under her breath.

"May I finish?" Ushag butted in. Ma stopped muttering and nodded. "There's only a little more. It's a small story as yet, but it'll grow as it goes.

"Among other things, the woman and the girl were tricked by this salamander," Auntie Ushag repeated, "and they had to strike a bargain with a water horse, but those are other stories from other times.

"Inside the earth palace was a pond. It had been chanted into being by the Invisibles who dwelled there, and its water sang eternally to them in the voices of seabirds and bubbles. The girl, with her bighearted-ness and true gaze, plainly heard the song telling them to trust the pond and they would be rewarded with a treasure more than gold, more than a strong body, more even than land. This woman, my friend, didn't hear any words. She only heard bubbling. Having misplaced the memories of her childhood, she now knew no treasures beyond those of grown people — gold, health, and land. She was suspicious of the calling water. The girl was not to be put off, though, and refused to go without her kinswoman, who then knew she must go whether she wanted to or not.

"After journeying through a tunnel of ice—where, by the way, the Invisibles tried to hold and drown them for the simple pleasure of new company—they rose into an upside-down room of that earth palace.

"All the lost memories come here to this topsy-turvy chamber, where they are put into pits and wait there for their owners to come and claim them. Not many come, so the pits are full to bursting. One of the pits holds lost memories of old journeys, in the shape of shoes. Another holds those of forgotten bothers in the form of flies; still another holds memories of mothers and sisters. The floors are salty from centuries of weeping, tears of both sorrow and pleasure.

"However, the biggest treasure of that journey hoard, for the woman of this story, was not to be a found memory but a new one. In that chamber of the earth palace, tending to the memory pits, lived an old merrow man, who seemed made up of only bones and coiling tail and dry cough. Once-silver, now-grey scales left a trail from pit to pit as he dragged his tail around the chamber. It knotted itself as he turned and turned from pit to pit, and he tripped over it many times a moment. The old male seemed to be shrinking, like one day he would shed his last scale and there he'd be: gone. His bed was already just a heap of his own scales.

"He found many of my friend's memories that

afternoon: childhood games and infant heartaches, great meals and foul meals, early songs and shell bangles, good friends made and lost, spats and enemies long forgotten, but the old merrow man will never know that he himself was the woman's greatest find. That's one memory will never end up in the pits.

"When life is hard, she just remembers the merrow man and his long, knotted tail to have all her happiness returned to her.

"That's the end." Ushag stopped and took up the jug and poured for us all. "What do you think?" There was nothing I could say, so I didn't. The glow of the bonfire was in me, and thunder rolled in from the cove. The starry night was losing its rule as storm clouds sailed in.

"I think it'll brush up nicely," said Ma. She toasted my aunt. "Especially with Scully to add the finer points. Like where that salamander comes in." She smiled in a meady haze, then her lip curled and her foot twitched like she was already kicking the evil thing in her mind's eye.

"Not salamanders again." Scully plucked at his fiddle strings, and as he did, one of its pegs dropped out. He started feeling for it in the grass around where he sat. "Maybe something more about the song of the pool, though . . ." His spider-fingers crept into the grass between us. Dreamy from the jug and the story,

I didn't notice him pick something up from beside me and fit it to his fiddle.

When he started the tune, though, straightaway I noticed, and everybody else too. The voice of his fiddle was changed. Its high notes had always rather scratched and pulled at the ears, though nobody minded, as Scully always managed to use the scratch to reach further into a body's heart. Everybody knows that fiddles have different voices, like people, but when he played that night, it was as if Ma had suddenly stood up and talked with the Prior's voice, or Bo had barked. Even Scully stopped for a moment before going on, his brow creased and his eyes blinking over and over.

The rest of us listened with shock turning to delight. This new voice was shy, but pure and glad. It filled the grove with all the good sounds, such as people laughing, night birds singing, or teeming rain outside when you're tucked up by the hearth in a rabbit-and-hare rug with nothing to do but stay there until it's over. As we listened, each one lifted his or her eyes to the sky and smiled. Scully played the short sweet tune all through, and stopped.

"Well, bugger me," he said, running his hands over the instrument, and then I saw. His old wooden peg was lying where it had fallen; he had fitted the fiddle with Mam's finger bone. Nobody had noticed, so I flicked the old peg into the dark beyond the firelight. A new life in Scully's fiddle seemed to me a good swap for that cold stone shelf in the sea cave.

Ulf rose and patted Scully's shoulder. *"Fagr Söngr."* He smiled before doing a little jig and winding through the grove toward the house, humming and muttering as he went. Ushag followed him.

"Pudding," she shouted over her shoulder at us. The rest of us sawed off the last bits of hare. Ma lifted part of hers to the fire before popping it into her mouth and sighing.

"This night is almost done for us," she said, pulling her shawl close and watching the sky. There was only a small dome of stars left in the middle of swarming cloud. "We don't have much time, and I have something to tell you young ones myself. I met another sort of hare today. Charmed it was, from the Other Place."

"Now, Mary . . ." started the Prior, but Ma cut him off.

"Don't 'Now, Mary' me, Father; I don't have time to fuss with you about such things. This hare, she had a message for me. According to her, I'm for passing over, and soon too. I've just got time to see my boy settled in the holding with his friends about him and sort out my dead dress, and then I'm for the West."

"Hares do not prophesy people's dying," stated the Prior, as simply as if he was only saying that one thing and another thing make two things. "And if they do, then it's not a hare. It's the Old Enemy come to lure simple, uneducated minds to corruption." He took the remains of the sea broth, piled roasted roots into it, and tucked in once more. You'd have thought they never fed him down at the Abbey.

"Well, that's all you know, and I'm sorry for it, but the charmed ones don't know they can't. They just do, and that's all. It's all up for me. And to tell the truth, I'm ready to rest in the memory of others . . . whether you want it to be so or not," Ma told him straight. "And who are you calling simple? My name's Mureal." The Prior seemed to lose his appetite, and put his trencher to one side. He took Ma's hand and entwined all his fingers with hers. There's nobody, mortal or Otherwise, who doesn't understand this kind of talk: the kind uttered by the body when words aren't working. The face on him was gloomy, and Ma wouldn't have it.

"When I die," she told him, leaving her hand in his, "there will be a great turnout and a knees-up. Scully will play his jigs. No sad tunes, my lad, all right?"

Scully nodded, calm and unchanged by Ma's news, at home as he was with all things Otherwise. It was as though she'd said she was going to Merton and would see him later. "After that, I will sail the western seas to the island where the souls of my other children wait for me. Some parts of them may be forever with Themselves in the Other Place, but their mother will find the more important parts of them and draw them in around her. I will wear my dead dress, with a rinse of lemons to brighten it and of rosemary to take away the smell of wormwood. I'll do that tomorrow.

"My boy and my girl will meet me on their shore, and I will embrace each one. Their faces will be as autumn apples to me, their gaze will fall like spring sunshine, and I will drink the nectar of their voices. Their breath will breathe upon the seared places of my heart, and I will be whole once more. The years will pass away, and I will stand in peace with the gods again. The lovely boy Jesus will be there, and he will feast with us."

"Now, really, don't be so foolish," said the Prior churlishly, taking his hand back, but Ma turned on him so quick and fixed him with such an eye that we all held our breath. He stopped talking straightaway.

Ma went on in her regular voice, kindly and old. "He has told me so, and who am I to not believe what he tells me?"

"Look here, I'm sorry, but the Lord Jesus Christ does not go around telling pagans He'll meet them in the western islands," insisted the Prior, though to me he seemed sorry for it. "The days of miracles, and of Him walking and talking with His own, are over.

Why would He talk to you if He doesn't talk to His very own?"

"Well, how do you know what He does and doesn't do if He doesn't talk to you?" I asked.

"I read my Bible, and I pray," he told me.

"What if you can't read?" This was Scully, his voice quiet and calm among the trees.

"Well, then . . ." said the Prior. "Then you must listen to those who can."

"To you, in fact," Scully suggested in a seemingly friendly manner.

We all looked at the Prior closely, like he was a book we could read.

"To me . . ." he trailed off. We looked at him even closer. He gave us a shaky smile.

"Why would I listen to somebody who doesn't even talk with Jesus?" said Ma, and that was that. The Prior gave up on us.

"Once I've got my sons and daughters all together again," went on Ma, "Jesus will take us up in his silvered drift nets, through the cloudy realm, and to his own Great Hall. There I will live with my children all together in a good, strong roundhouse, and we will till the paradise fields until they yield to us wild strawberries and sweet wine. And Scully will have somewhere to come when it's his time, he won't have to return to the Halls of the Others. Jesus's Father will keep us safe from Themselves, and old Breeshey will come to talk and story with us. All the gods will be pleased with me again, and I'll be able to rest."

I put my arms around her and touched my hot cheek to her cool one, as dry and veined as a leaf. "What god could be angry with you?" I said.

Ma sighed. "Take your pick," she answered me. "I was beside myself with the lot of them for years. I called them names such as no decent person should even overhear for fear of soul rot on the back of it. I crossed the bones at them and cursed them daily. My praying was often only so much name-calling and moans. My best prayer was only a prayer to be able to pray again." She thumped at her chest and sat up. "But they still put the heart in me to go on. No limping, fair-weather gods in Carrick, only those who talk to a body in their own way and help her to live and find life good after all."

Truly, that old woman was a marvel, and I wouldn't be surprised if, when I pass, I find all is exactly as she said.

Scully picked up his fiddle, and my mother's voice filled the hazel grove, singing at our fireside as was only right. I went into the dark to piss, and as I did so, I saw Ulf and Ushag coming back with the pudding. Suddenly I was hungry for sweetness, for all the honey, figs, mint, or whatever was in that dish they carried between them. Leaping up, I ran toward them in the dark. That pudding looked heavy, it looked sizable, and I couldn't wait.

Then they stopped, and for some reason, so did I. Their faces under the swift clouds were like twin moons. Ulf stooped to her, and their brows touched over the pudding. Ulf was whispering to my aunt in his own talk, and she was watching his mouth with a face on her I'd never seen. The face was so Otherwise, I even looked away once, but as I think I've said before, I learn too much by eavesdropping and I wasn't about to stop now. I opened them again.

She had closed her eyes and was shaking her head. He kept on whispering—in fact, he started hissing—but she folded her arms and looked at him so straight, he stopped straightaway. They stood for a moment with the early raindrops spitting and steaming about them; then he stopped and stuck his hand into the pudding. When he pulled it out, he was holding a pearl, as big as a wild plum and glowing like the moon in his hand. Ushag looked at it like she'd never seen one before. I could hear Ulf, the wind, and the night all hold their breath. Then she looked up, and the light of the pearl was in her eyes.

Ulf laughed then. Picking her up by the waist with one arm, and with the pudding in his other hand, he stumbled toward the hazels with Ushag seeming tinier than I'd ever seen her, and kicking fit to bust. Her kicking wasn't real, though, it was some type of play, and I felt strange about seeing it, so I turned away. Whatever it was, the thing between Ulf and Auntie Ushag was bound to change everything.

Back at the fire, everybody cheered the arrival of the pudding. It turned out to be somewhat of a tower of wine-soaked figs, almonds, and spiced cakes, spotted over with mint, fennel seed, and violets. The top battlement of the tower was formed of stuffed apples, and the whole dripped in butter and honey. It was a little hollowed out after Ulf's hand had been stuck into it, but to me it was still like a dream of food, as Ushag was like a dream of my aunt.

Before finding the merrow bones, my aunt would never have thought of hosting a feast and wouldn't have fed the Prior if he'd turned up starving. She'd have been after him with the broom at first sight of him in the cove. She would have enjoyed it, and so would I. Before the proving of the merrows, she would never have let the blue man stay in Marrey Cove, never mind opening the wreck trunk for him. Once he was able to walk, he'd have been sent off to live or die among the southerners—in towns now busy ridding themselves of outsiders and monsters to be ready for their end-of-the-world.

Now, freed from her story, she could take her

enemy's hand. Freed from her own story, she could be kind to strangers.

"I tell you what, Father," she said now, putting her hand on his shoulder. He flinched like he'd expected her to slap him. "When that Christian sky of yours falls, we'll all just go catch larks." And she held out to him, shining with butter and honey, the first of the stuffed apples from the top of the tower of pudding.

I knew then. I would never tell her.

CHAPTER NINETEEN

Go Tell the Bees

I HAD TO TELL SOMEBODY.

Three days after the feast, my new knowledge was harrowing my mind and burning on my tongue. I could have told Scully, but he was to be my first and best ally in the saving of Ushag from herself. In him the story of the merrows of Marrey Cove rose smooth and honey-tongued, and given the chance, he could persuade the pearl from the shell. I needed him to keep faith. I couldn't tell Ma; she had enough to be going on with, what with the prophecy of her own death and all. Her dead dress lay airing over the berry canes by their threshold, like a pile of glossy ravens with their black feathers stirring stiffly in a breeze. The Prior was impossible, and Ulf wouldn't understand—or perhaps he'd understand the story, but not the secret. Some people think that facts are the only truth. He might think it dishonorable or something, and think it only right to tell my aunt about her own sister's bones. But if he was to keep his new friend, Ushag needed to keep the merrows, and that was that. Some stories are truer than facts.

I had to tell somebody, but it had to be somebody who wouldn't, or couldn't, tell Ushag. I settled on the bees. Scully had said they were Marrey bees, so in a way they were family.

Bo and I set ourselves for the hawthorn grove. It had rained for two days after Ushag's feast, and the earth was soft and brown again. The heat had broken that night, and our holiday scattered by storms. As the first fat singular drops had fallen, we'd let them hit us full in the face. They'd hissed and steamed as they hit the feverish ground. All the barrels filled in a half hour, and the water was still running away in trickles, streams, and torrents down to the sea. Since then, we'd had two more days of sheet rain, and though for now the black sky towers in the cove were holding off, we could smell that it wouldn't be for long. All the smells that had lain locked in the dust all summer were now at their liberty in the cooling air. My breath prickled with sharp goodness.

As we left the yard, Bo trotted right beside me in a lather of mud and gladness, leaning against me like a hound and with such weight I was nearly knocked off my feet. I rested my hand on her neck as we went and breathed in the byre: the fresh dung, the straw, and her own warm hide. I was eased to have her with me, even if she was just a cow.

Up in the grove, the bees were all abuzz. They, too, could smell the rains returning. Their king had put them all to their tasks before it broke, as Ushag and Ulf were even now readying our place for flooding and drenching. I had left them hurriedly packing the walls with straw and fortifying the roof as I sloshed up toward the hazels and the grove of bees. The embroidered curtains from the wreck trunk flapped wetly as I passed between them, and the tapestries seemed already just part of the soil.

Now, I didn't know how to go about actually telling the bees. Auntie Ushag and I didn't do that sort of thing. Ma was the only person I knew who talked to creatures like they were folk, and often to folk like they were creatures, but somehow I didn't want to ask. You can't ask your family to talk to the bees for you. It's something a person has to manage for themselves. I sat by the hives and listened to that busy world for some time.

At last I lay my gift of a leftover currant-stuffed apple by the biggest hive in the grove and greeted what I hoped was the bee king.

"Blessings on you, little minister of sweetness," I

started, and was pleased with the tone I struck, which managed to sound both respectful and friendly, and the bees themselves hummed louder, so I was encouraged. "I come to bring thankfulness for your labor all these years of the cove, and to tell you of a passing," I said. A cold gust blew through the grove, and there was silence. I leaned forward and lay my head against the trunk by the hive. Now I was unsure how to say what I had to say.

"Your mistress has turned up dead," I whispered. Some of the bees had found the gift and were dancing in the wet grass. Others followed to see what the fuss was about. The buzz grew until the whole grove hummed and sang, and it seemed like the whole hive town crowded into that sweet, stuffed apple. They had accepted the gift. They would not be leaving the cove yet. "She lies drowned on a shelf in the cliff," I told them.

My words weren't enough. A person's life should add up to more words than nine. All those words I'd been told about Mam over the years—all wrong, or only partly right, or just plain nasty. All those stories that weren't hers anymore, or mine. Even the merrow story had passed from me and now lived in Ushag. She needed it more than I did. Meanwhile, I felt like a fish out of water without it. I felt unclothed, cold, and alone without a story for Mam and me.

If I didn't make my own story, there were plenty to do it for me. Some would do it kindly, others any way they could, but I knew now I wouldn't like it. What I needed was a new story, the right story to say what I knew about Mam; I needed a story in which both lies and facts could turn to truth in my throat.

The events of that overhot summer were leeching from my memory. That day in the grove between the rains, I could hardly remember the start of our sky-clad season: something about heat, something about seals and scales, and something about the truth is all I recalled. What I needed was my own, my very own, story. One that would lie like a reptile on the hot rock of my heart and tell others to go away.

"My mother was a little wild, like all of us who live in lonely places," I started, and my voice was like a mild wind, quiet but everywhere in the grove at once. Like the honey-tongued Slevins when they told the Other stories, or like the Prior when he talked about the end of the world, the story told itself. "She sang of salt and rock and water, and she was brave and true. She wed for love, not dirt or work, and her husband was young and strong before being taken in honor to serve the kraken in his Court. My mother conceived me in hope and cheerfulness, and we had three years together before . . ."

Before what? I thought. This story making was a

slippery thing. I needed something that was true about her, or it wouldn't work. Everything turns into a story the moment it's done. The facts of things do not store well. They rot and fall apart. But the stories we tell last and even grow. What was to be the truth of her death?

She could have drowned herself, as Ushag said.

She could have been dragged off course, as I was, and then drowned by the changeable tides and tows of the cove.

She could have retreated into the caves and died there from the ice-and-salt elements.

She could even have been murdered, as some say down south. I didn't think so, though. I just knew, like Ma. I started up again.

"A daughter knows her own mam," I told the bees. "The scaly skin covers us both, and her face lives in my face. Her blood runs through me. Her bones live only in my memory."

That was good. It sounded right and true. Ma had said that's where bones lie. I carried on.

"A northerner knows their own cove. My mother still lives in the sand where she played as a child and with her child, and up the cliff path where she walked. The byre holds the buckets she filled and mended, and the orchard brims with her sweetness. We still eat from her work and bless her sweat. We tell her stories to each other, and we even fight over her.

"She is still with us, in spite of those who tried to steal her. They tried to steal her with enchanted words tucked in stories. The hid her in Mirror tales, which only reflect the longings and dooms of the listeners. They made her invisible in Vanishing tales, and pocked her all over with evil in Splatter tales. They thought to hide her in one of those stories from the long dark of midwinter, spiked with murder and the Old Enemy.

"There are always folk in need of other folk to flesh out their own stories. They need others to join in before they can believe in anything at all. They commonly get about in crowds and tend to ganging up. During her troubles, under siege and unprotected, they robbed Ven from us to trap her alive in a bad story. In spite of it all, I always knew her. I saw her through those lies.

"A daughter knows.

"My mother was as full of stories as a spring pilchard is of eggs. After the death of Colm Breda, though, she lost herself in that one story: the story of Lost Love. She was a shelled crab after that, soft and easy to the teeth. For a year and a day, she walked Carrick among its everyday cruelty. A year and a day she ripped her tunic and covered her breast in ashes; a year and a day she wept, salting her meal with tears. Then one morning, a morning that dawned like the first morning of the world, she tired of that story and stopped weeping. She felt herself changed. Somewhere deep in the veins and caverns of her body, a new thing was growing and thriving.

"Longing for the scour of the salt and the shock of water, she took me and went to the shore. She waded into the quicksilver sea. Brimful with the new thing, she turned, lightclad, to smile at me. Her body went as the High Lake on a bright day. It ruffled. Then she turned to face the horizon.

"Her mortal body became a ribbon of sparks that moved over the water, at first holding its form, then loosening and flying apart like a pack of swallows startled in a field. At the last, she dropped in atoms and specks, fathoms deep into the kelp forest, where she has become the new thing she felt inside her body.

"Her waving hair is plaited through the wrack, her many eyes flash about the seabed, her fingers idle among the anemone gardens, and her lips talk with clams as they were never able to talk with folk. Her voice is in the wind, her ears in the sea caves, and her heart beats in my stone sack. Instead of carrying the stories, the stories now carry her. She is a wake.

"The fact is that on that day in the cove, my mother turned to stories. People can do that. What is anybody in the end but the story of themselves?

"She lives in Scully's fiddle and the new tune he made on the feast night. She lives in the secret silver hoops on a hidden rock shelf. She lives by Ma's hearth, where she sat the Slevins through their troubles. Like it or not, she still lives in Market-Shipton, where they never before saw her kind and are still trying to tell the story of it over their grog and envy.

"And she lives in Auntie Ushag, the only aunt left in Marrey Cove, the aunt who stayed."

Now, that is a true story. I'm sticking to it. Honor Bright.

Glossary

bodge — old timber; [adj.: bodgey]

cronk [Manx] — hill

earwig — eavesdropping person

grog blossom [Manx] — a red nose from constant drunkenness

hedge pig — hedgehog

heishan [Manx] — half-grown girl; hoyden

kraken — sea monster, something like a huge octopus

longtail [Manx] — rat

merrow — mermaid

moaney [Manx] — peatland, bog

wiggynagh [Manx] — raider or viking